ALMOST A HOLIDAY

ALMOST
A HOLIDAY

BRENDAN MULHOLLAND

Illustrated by Trog

MACMILLAN
London · Melbourne · Toronto

1966

01077561

Text © Brendan Mulholland 1966
Illustrations © Macmillan & Co. Ltd 1966

MACMILLAN AND COMPANY LIMITED
Little Essex Street London WC2
also Bombay Calcutta Madras Melbourne

THE MACMILLAN COMPANY OF CANADA LIMITED
70 Bond Street Toronto 2

ST MARTIN'S PRESS INC
175 Fifth Avenue New York NY 10010

PRINTED IN GREAT BRITAIN BY
NORTHUMBERLAND PRESS LIMITED
GATESHEAD ON TYNE

TO MY WIFE

AUTHOR'S NOTE

Once in a pub I listened to a conversation between a man and a woman. They agreed that hanging was too good for somebody they had read about in the newspaper but the woman, who almost visibly bounced in her seat with rage, went farther. She said the person in the newspaper should be locked in a cell without windows and light and kept alive on bread and water and never, ever let out. The man agreed with her.

I was one of the two newspaper reporters who went to prison in 1963 for refusing to reveal my sources of information to the Radcliffe Tribunal which was set up after an Admiralty clerk called Vassall was convicted and jailed as a spy. I served five days in a closed prison and the balance of four months in an open prison — a 'prison without bars'.

People on the outside looking in on such prisons have described them as holiday camps. The inmates themselves have been known to say much the same thing, though perhaps in a different tone of voice. As with most things it is the point of view that counts.

The prison in this story does not exist. Neither do the

prisoners nor the people in charge of them. The events themselves are fictitious.

What is real is the anger which builds up in a man whose liberty has been taken away. The men in this story are not in blackened cells and they are not fed on bread and water. Yet each one is as alone as if he were.

They live in a world totally lacking in *esprit de corps* and in the end the mistrust and the anger injure their minds as surely as the blackness and the loneliness.

There may be no answer to the problem. Criminals must be punished and dangerous men must be kept off the streets. But I once met a man doing four years for stealing a hairbrush from Woolworth's. He had done it twenty-two times before and the Judge said he must be taught a lesson. A week after he was released he stole his twenty-fourth hairbrush.

Perhaps you cannot teach a man not to fight by beating his head. You may just make him a dirtier fighter.

I have no answer to the problem; perhaps there isn't one. But I do know it is high time we looked.

B. M.

CHAPTER 1

James Hubert Markham came awake with the sun on his face. The light, thin and piercing, slanted through the wire mesh some yards beyond his window and cast a pattern of misshapen diamonds on his skin and the yellow wall beyond his bed. The skin was grey and very old, wrinkled on the face but smooth and hairless where ill-fitting pyjamas revealed part of his chest.

James screwed his eyes up against the light, seeing nothing but a vivid wall of red, flashing with white lights. He listened to the thumping of his heart and held himself rigid, fearful that if he moved his chest would burst. The thumping grew more violent and then began to die down with intermittent flutterings causing the old man to gulp for extra air. Gradually it steadied and he relaxed the tension in his limbs, feeling as though he were sinking deeper into the hard mattress. Slowly he opened his eyes and saw the blurred outline of the window and the handbasin to the left and they began to come into focus as he watched.

The sky was pale blue with wisps and balls of dusty cloud. He could see the roof of the main gatehouse and the top of the wire fence, four strands of barbed wire set in at an angle from the fence itself. There was the noise of clattering cans in the distance and the voices of the men taking breakfast to the other compounds. The wind made a low moaning sound as it passed through the wires. Did that wind never stop? James closed his eyes again feeling a terrible misery creeping into him. It had been like this for more than a year now, the awakening with the near certainty that he was about to die and then, after a moment of relief, the thought that he would be better off dead.

The thumpings in his chest had been worse this morning, and the following morning they would be worse again. Only three months to go and he was not going to make it. A picture of Jane flashed into his mind, Jane in a pretty smock pruning roses in their garden. The old man tried to push it out of his mind, forcing other thoughts in: the book he had been reading the night before; the final of the snooker competition he had to play tonight. The picture of Jane flashed in and out of his thoughts and now a picture of Tom at the bar of the 'Barley Mow'. Good old Tom. He was doing everything he could.

The misery subsided quickly. Tom and Jane would get him out. The old man had seen a picture of the Home Secretary in the paper a few days ago and he looked a kindly man no matter what everybody said about him. The Governor might know something today and Jane and Tom were coming in Billy's car. The old man relaxed again. He would give himself another two minutes and then he would get up. The sun was warm through the window and he felt comfortable. He counted off the seconds slowly, listening to the increasing noise in the corridor outside his room, the obscene words from Sam's room on his right and Bert's grating cough to his left.

Bert was a baron and he smoked a lot. He hammered on the thin wall between the two rooms. 'Up you get, Jimmy!' Bert went off into another fit of coughing. The old man heard Bert's door open and the coughing fade away towards the lavatory at the bottom. He called back 'Thanks!' and eased himself into a sitting position, sliding his feet slowly on to the floor and feeling the thumping in his chest begin again. He sat still for a few seconds while it died down and pushed himself up, his thin, cranky old legs quivering with effort. Again he waited for a few seconds to allow himself to become accustomed to his new position, then he stooped slowly and pulled his slippers from under the bed. The slippers went out of focus and disappeared as a blackness came over the old man's eyes. He sat down quickly on the edge of the bed and waited for his head to clear, feeling for his carefully-folded vest with his left hand and pulling it on while he waited with his eyes closed. A few seconds and he would be all right.

There it was. He hummed a tune as he pulled his trousers on over his pyjama pants and tucked the bottom of the pants into his socks. It might be spring but that wind could still be chilly. Better be on the safe side. The old man stood up again and shuffled across to the handbasin, his slippers, made out of an old blanket and soled with slabs of matted string, clomping on the wooden floor as they fell away from his heels. His razor was laid out neatly in three pieces on the shelf above the basin and his blade by the side of it, always kept carefully wrapped in its paper. The old man looked in the mirror at the grey stubble, rubbing his hand over it. Day five; it would be a medium-to-tough shave today. Perhaps he would be out before the next issue of blades on Sunday. He felt cheerful as he lathered his face with the discoloured soap packed tightly into an old Brylcreem jar. Bert had done that for him. He had collected dozens of small pieces of soap to make this shaving-mug.

The old man shaved one side of his face, the old blade pulling slightly at the whiskers. Then he rested. He put down his razor and massaged the inside of his right arm with his other hand to ease the pain where the sinews felt as though they had been knotted together. He

4

shaved his upper lip and his chin and rested again, fitting his false teeth into his mouth while he waited for the pain in his right arm to go away.

Bert was coughing back up the corridor. Sam was moving about on the other side, cursing away to himself. He finished every sentence with 'didn't I?' and almost every other word was a profanity. 'So I crippled the poxy bastard, didn't I?' the old man heard Sam say with sudden vehemence. Then there was a crashing sound as something fell into the handbasin in the next room and more profanities.

The old man's door opened and Bert pushed his bald head into the room, a friendly, toothless grin on his face. It was a big face with big lips, big nose and huge sagging jowls covered now with a black stubble. He wore only pyjama trousers which reached to just below his knees and left a foot-wide gap at the front through which part of his enormous belly protruded. The old man wished that Bert would not walk around like that. He could easily have put his trousers on before he left his room.

'All right, Jimmy?' Bert asked. 'How's the shaving going?' He had a strong North Country accent and he said everything at the top of his voice. The old man had been told that he was doing five and had three to go but Bert never spoke about it himself.

'Fine thank you', the old man said, smiling. 'Nearly finished.' Bert closed the door with a crash and stamped back into his own room slamming his door behind him.

'Noisy whoring bastard!' Sam called from the other side.

The old man finished his shave and sat down on the edge of the bed to put his shoes on, heavy, black shoes which were unequal in size and chafed his heels. His socks had shrunk, leaving the heels under the arches of his feet. By the end of the day they would probably have disappeared completely into his shoes. He stood up and put his shirt on. It cut him under the arms and the collar was too small, making it impossible for him to fasten the top button. He knotted his black tie, shiny with constant use, using the knot to hide the gap in the collar left at his throat. His jacket hung neatly over a chair at the bottom of his bed and his long brown raincoat beside it on a peg on the wall. Perhaps it was warm enough to go without the coat today. He would go out in a moment and see.

The old man took a bundle of letters from one of the breast pockets of his jacket and sat down on a chair. He took one of the letters out of the elastic band holding them together and read the first few lines.

'Dear Jimmy, How are you, darling? You have no idea how much I miss you. The spring flowers are out now in the garden and everything looks wonderful. But I cannot enjoy it when you are not here with me. . . . Tom and the vicar have written to the Home Secretary and we are hoping . . .'

The old man read no further, knowing that lower down the page Jane had cautioned him not to let his hopes rise too high. He had read the letter a dozen times but at this moment he wanted nothing to dull his optimism. He tucked the letter back under the band and put the bundle back into his jacket pocket. The Home Secretary had a wife and children. He would realise that it was all so pointless. After all there were only three months left and he was a sick man as the doctor here could testify.

The old man buttoned on his jacket and went out into the corridor, feeling the heels of his socks digging into his soles. There was a draught blowing down the corridor from the big window open at one end but it was a warmish draught. The old man felt sure he would be comfortable enough without his raincoat today especially as the forecast on television the night before had been sunny with moderate south-easterly winds. The man from the room opposite was leaning in his open doorway, still unshaven and with his shirt unbuttoned to the waist. He had pale, staring eyes and a sneering mouth and he made no response at all to Jimmy's 'Good morning'. The old man had seen him arrive from the Scrubs two days before, a shambling bundle of rags tied together by string at the waist, the ankles, and wrists, every article of clothing on his back patched and better-patched until it was difficult to tell what began life as what. The man had had a beard then, matted with dirt. His skin was ingrained with dirt which looked as though it would never come out. The screws had made a bonfire of the rags behind the dining-hall and the man had been steeped in a hot bath. The old man had not recognised him for some minutes the next time he saw him. That was at the clothing store when the man had heaped abuse on the screw in charge because he was given a shirt which did not fit and a jacket with a stain on one of the sleeves. The old man hurried past the man in the doorway and down to the lavatory where Old George was brewing tea in an old jam tin.

Old George, who was only about forty, had made himself an immersion heater out of two strands of copper wire, one attached to the side of the tin and the other fixed to a small tin lid suspended in the water from a stick resting across the top of the jam tin. The other ends of the wires were plugged with matchsticks into a wall-socket. The old man handed Old George his cup and Old George filled it with watery tea. Bert came into the lavatory and Old George filled his cup. Then Sam came in, a shambling little man with red-raw eyes that blinked madness, and a mouth wet with saliva.

'Told the bastard, didn't I?' said Sam. 'Poxy shit-house.' Nobody replied but the old man smiled at Sam, who would not have understood a reply anyway.

Another man came into the lavatory with his cup and pushed it towards Old George but Bert put his arm up and pushed the man away. 'Piss off, Jackson,' he said. 'Pay me that quarter you owe me and you might get something.'

The old man was embarrassed because Jackson cleaned his room for him for an ounce of tobacco a week. He knew that Jackson owed Bert a quarter and that Bert would get it one way or another. He emptied the dregs from his cup into one of the toilets and edged towards the door. 'See you at breakfast.' He escaped quickly into the corridor and walked out through the swing doors at the end, through the hallway where the clock said twenty-five minutes past six, and out into the sunshine.

There was a heavy feeling in his chest and his right arm still ached from shaving. He could also feel a pain in his right thigh he could not remember before. The thick wire mesh, fifteen feet high, stretched away in front of him with, at one end, the heavy gates with the double lock they said was unbreakable. Beyond the gates the screws were arriving in their cars, wearing white jackets now because the weather was warmer. Some of them brought their children as far as the gate then the children walked on up the road to school.

The old man thought of Billy and the day he and Jane had taken their son to his first prep school. Billy had done well. A success in the City and married to a young woman whose father would one day leave her a fortune. Her father had visited him once at the beginning but he had never come again and he had not written. Billy came nearly every month but never with his wife. The old man shook off the thought and began to walk along by the wire with the sun on his back. Yes, he would be all right without his raincoat today.

The old man heard the voices behind him before he

heard the footsteps of the two men, the kind of well-bred voices that could cut their way through a hurricane. He tried to quicken his step but the pain in his thigh was too much. Then one of the followers called out 'Morning, Markham, old man,' and he slowed down to let them catch up. The two men, both fat and bald-headed, drew level and fell in step with him.

One said: 'Jeremy was just suggesting a rubber of bridge tonight. How about you, James?' The old man could feel the nerves in his finger ends twitch. Good God, where did they think they were, some sort of country club?

'Philip and I want our revenge, you know,' said Jeremy in his penetrating drawl. The old man muttered that he was playing in the snooker final.

God damn it, these two were worse than Sam with their bridge and chess and their arguments in the library about who should be first with *Paris-Match* and *The Times Literary Supplement*. They name-dropped endlessly and handed their matchstick-thin roll-ups to each other in some sort of desperate attempt to preserve a way of life the old man was sure they had never known. Probably arrived at the Scrubs like that rag-bag in the room opposite and put on their prison uniforms like some sort of old school tie. The old man could never once remember these two even mentioning where they were, let alone why they were there. It was like this every morning. They talked over their activities for the day as though they had a choice in the matter.

They both worked in one of the stores yet they referred to it as 'the office'. Damn them to hell, thought the old man, they're not even human enough to complain.

He tried to shut out their monotonous voices as they turned the corner and headed down the other side of the compound. Only two hundred yards and they would be outside the door to the main dining-hall and he could escape. They passed the lines of tiny vegetable plots, almost all of them filled with lettuce and radish. On some of the plots were tomato- and cucumber-frames, pathetic, home-made affairs constructed of wood and pieces of ill-fitting polythene most of which had been torn by the wind. A few men were working on their plots digging in the dry, stony ground with makeshift tools. The trio stopped by Sam's plot where Sam was mouthing obscenities over a heap of broken wood and shredded polythene to which the wind had reduced his cucumber-frame during the night.

'Damn vandals, I suppose,' said Jeremy and turned away clucking in disgust. The old man felt like kicking him.

Farther along they stopped by another plot where a tall, thin man was hoeing between immaculate rows of lettuce. At the back of his plot he had constructed a large tomato-frame out of wood and glass. Inside the frame were six huge tomato plants with dozens of small green tomatoes already showing.

Philip and Jeremy discussed the plot loudly, remarking on the quality of the 'crop' and repeating how nicely a lettuce would go down with Sunday tea. Their own plot, a particularly stony one nearby, had produced nothing so far and did not look like doing so in the future. The thin man waved his hoe at them threateningly and shouted at them to go away. Somebody had trampled on the thin man's plot some days before and the old man knew he suspected his two companions. They said the thin man had done time in Parkhurst and in Dartmoor and that when he found out who had trampled his plants he would cripple them. The old man moved away feeling his cheerfulness ebbing. The weight on his chest seemed heavier and his right leg felt stiff. The other two turned in at the entrance to the dining-hall but the old man walked on wanting nothing but to be left alone.

The sun shone warmly on his face and he quickened his stride to try to loosen the stiffness in his leg. Through the wire in one of the other compounds he could see the men from the kitchen pushing the big barrow with the gleaming tureens of porridge across to the wooden dining-hall. They joked noisily with the screw who accompanied them and pushed at each other playfully. From all over the prison, men streamed towards the dining-halls in twos and threes, grim-faced mostly and with their eyes on the ground. A group of eight men were walking down past the sports ground to the main gate dressed in their civilian clothes and carrying their blankets and prison clothes with them to be handed in at the gatehouse. The old man went closer to the wire

to see if he could recognise any of the men who were
being freed. Several of them were well dressed but a
couple were particularly shabby and he recognised one
of them as a rather pleasant young man who had
worked in the main offices. You could never tell in here,
he thought. Everybody looks alike in the uniforms. The
worst and the best are equal because everybody is nothing. The breakfast bell clanged loudly and the old man
turned back towards the dining-hall.

The wind blew his thick, grey hair into a spike on
top of his head. James Hubert Markham, from office boy
to stockbroker to nothing in threescore-odd years, going
in to breakfast after an early morning stroll. The Judge
had dealt with a thousand like him, spitting out the
established invective selected from the tool kit of his
mind as he looked down at the job on the conveyor
belt below. One old man in running order, but only just;
bodywork clean. Moral fibre badly worn, clutch on life
slipping. A bad case of wanton disregard for the property of others, an abuse of trust, a man in your position
handling the affairs of dozens of small investors, greed,
turpitude, attempts to conceal, age no excuse, did make
some attempt to put things right but . . . must be
punished. Three years and three years and three years
to run concurrently. Court adjourned until two o'clock,
lunch at the Devereux, golf tomorrow. That tricky
what's-his-name case on Monday.

Jane had screamed, a half-strangled scream that had
startled the old man out of the trance into which he

had been bludgeoned by words. A man in uniform had led him gently by the arm down the narrow, wooden stairs to the cells where Jane and Tom were waiting for him to talk of appeals to the High Court and the House of Lords and even the Archbishop of Canterbury, but the old man heard little of what they said. They put him in a tiny cubicle in a prison van and drove him to Wormwood Scrubs where they slammed the big gate behind him and put him to wait with fifty other men of all ages and sizes and conditions and personalities. When his turn came the old man was taken into another room to see the doctor, who looked at his throat, listened to his heart and felt his testicles, without once looking into his face.

Nobody spoke, not even the kindly-looking prison officer who led him to the bath house and motioned him to take off his clothes and climb into one of the baths which held four inches of lukewarm water. The old man wished he were dead. Afterwards they gave him a brown uniform to wear and took him back to the room where he had waited with the fifty other different men and now the men were all the same. Prison officers walked briskly through the room from all directions, the big chains holding their keys slapping against their thighs. They cut brown men out from the herd without a word and moved away with them in silence like creatures in a dream. When the old man's turn came, he walked with four other prisoners behind two officers out of the room into the damp September air. The high walls glistened with moisture. By one of the walls a hundred or so men shuffled round and round in a small circle, walking in pairs, smoking and talking quietly. They walked into one of the huge cell blocks with its tiers of cells just like the old man had seen at the pictures, terrifying rows of doors behind which were God-knows-what manner of animal.

The block was alive with noise, the clatter of tin plates and the hum of voices and every now and then a loud curse or grating laughter which had nothing to do with fun. They opened one of the doors for the old man and he stepped inside. Two men were in the cell, lying on their bunks smoking thin cigarettes. The cell smelled of tobacco, stale urine and sweat and as the old man flopped down on to his bed a cloud of dust rose from the thin mattress. There was a barred window high in the outside wall and a tiny peep-hole in the steel door. Underneath the peep-hole somebody had written: 'Don't put your head out of the window, the last man got stuck.' The walls of the cell were covered with filthy scribblings, the vilest, most intimate details of wives and lovers whose men had been locked in a steel and concrete box with only a piece of pencil and a wall on which to express their anger and their longings. The old man lay on his back with his eyes closed, listening with a terrible fear to the banging of cell doors as other human beings were locked away. Somebody was banging with a spoon on one of the heating pipes and singing in a flat voice.

One of the other men climbed down from his bunk, dropped his trousers and sat on his chamber-pot, still chatting to his companion. The old man turned his face to the wall feeling tears of misery come into his eyes.

Three months and two days the old man slept in that bed until the smell became part of everything, along with the sight of grown men sitting like babies on chamber-pots and queueing in the morning to empty the contents down the big drain outside. For a while he refused to use prison slang but in here he soon realised that it was not a good thing to be different, to call a screw a 'prison officer' or snout 'tobacco'. He came to accept the terrible violence as something which was nothing to do with him so long as he minded his own business and agreed with everybody. They put him to work in the library, printing hundreds of cards reminding prisoners that books were their best friends, and sorting through piles of mutilated volumes whose friendship had been brutally rejected. Existence fell into a pattern in which the best state of mind was indifference, the best part of each twenty-four hours' unconsciousness. Jane and Billy and Tom, and the world outside were not real any more. The men around him were real, happy men, sad men, vicious and gentle, and innocent to a man. They taught him a part of life he had never known existed: police brutality; crooked Judges; men beaten to death by screws in their peters; petitions to the Home Secretary torn up by the Governor; wives and sweethearts framed by the courts.

And were they not right? Where was the man in here without an alibi, an excuse, a hundred reasons why he couldn't have been at the warehouse when the night-watchman was coshed, an eye-witness who had sworn to the fact that he was in Scunthorpe at the time? Days ran into nights and nights into days as if light and dark were all the same and the old man, who had pleaded guilty before the Judge, had been railroaded to hell by a biased prosecuting counsel and a magistrate who would not listen to reason.

There were men who had been to prison before and boasted about it, but never a one who was inside legitimately this time. The old man had no sorrow to spare for these men but he knew that British justice was bad and that virtue was not its own reward. He worked and slept and ate, and listened to their stories, and always he knew, no matter what, that he was better than them.

Jane and Bill and Tom had each sent him a Christmas card, which he had been allowed to keep in his cell. It was snowing outside the day he was taken across to the Governor's office and told that he was being moved to an open prison where only first offenders and men who had no record of violence were kept. He and a dozen others were driven there in a coach through snowy country lanes past busy country hotels with expensive cars parked outside. The air, whipping in through an open window in the coach, was cold and clean. The old man felt glad to be alive. He thought of Jane at their cottage and hoped she had got in enough coal for the winter. It looked like being a cold one.

His City suit felt light and comfortable after the heavy prison uniform. The old man chatted amiably with his companions about what they would find when they arrived, pleased with themselves that the authorities had recognised them as men who could be trusted. They drove in through the main gates of the open prison and were met by the Governor and the chief prison-officer, both chubby, amiable-looking men. The Governor assured them they would be made comfortable if they worked well and behaved themselves. The old man was given one of the single rooms in the large block and assigned to work in one of the stores.

One year, five months and twenty-eight days ago. Two winters, two springs and one summer ago. One summer to go and the old man felt death at his elbow every morning.

The air had been fresh and clean that first January and bone-aching cold. The snow had piled feet-high but they had gone to work every morning at seven o'clock, the lashing wind cutting through their cheap raincoats and turning their hands to useless slabs of red meat. There had been no banter in the line-up as they waited to be marched to work outside the main block in those days. The men marched in grey-faced lines bracing themselves against the wind, the old man at the head of the column to open the tool store for the men working on the farm. Five hundred yards of torture six days a week and the old man did not care if he lived or died. Then the spring and the sunshine and the flowers. The men left their raincoats behind and told coarse jokes as they waited to march to work. The screws said that this was better than a holiday camp and everybody laughed easily.

The old man felt content despite the nagging pain he was beginning to get in his chest. It was a hot summer, sapping the energy from his limbs. He had appealed to the High Court against conviction and sentence and his appeal had been rejected. For a while he again wished himself dead, but then Jane and Tom wrote to say they were going to appeal directly to the Home Secretary. They would enlist the aid of the vicar and their family doctor and they seemed so full of confidence the old man's spirits were bucked a little. Another winter went by slowly, not so cold as the last. Jane and Tom were getting up a petition to present to the Archbishop of Canterbury and the Home Secretary which should be ready to send off soon. They had over 200 signatures, including two well-known authors.

Now it was spring again and Jane and Tom had written to say that they expected word soon from the Home Secretary, who was on holiday at the moment. But the pains were worse in the old man's chest. Just one day at home in their cottage with Jane, twenty-four hours of life before his Maker took him. It was not too much to ask, thought the old man wearily as he walked towards the dining-hall. What had he done to deserve this? Nothing. He had not been stealing those titles, anybody with half a brain could see that. The Judge just wouldn't listen. He pushed the injustice of it all out of his mind, trying to think how he would greet Jane and Tom when they arrived this afternoon. But anger kept butting in. What the hell did they care about an old man nicely locked up out of harm's way. They were probably having a good time for themselves on the way here. They would stop somewhere nice for lunch, no doubt, with wine and perhaps a liqueur afterwards and then they would have the gall to weep all over him when they arrived. They had been five minutes late last time and the old man, watching from behind the fence, had seen them laughing together as they went into the visitors' room. The old man turned through the hallway towards the dining-hall, ignoring Bert's 'Hello, Jimmy' as he passed the bottom of the stairs. Loud-mouthed bastard, could he never leave anybody alone? Always shouting and walking around half-naked. The old man, wishing his family and friends in hell, went in to breakfast.

CHAPTER 2

Harry, the porridge man, could be heard even above the pandemonium of eight hundred human beings cursing, eating, and dropping aluminium trays in an enclosed space some hundred feet long by fifty wide. Like Sam, Harry cursed non-stop and he was living proof that a sentence can be compounded without a verb. In fact Harry could at the drop of a hat produce a sentence made up entirely of adjectives, and frequently did.

Harry was arguing with a man called Dick, an enormous, evil-tempered man whose backside was so broad he had had to have gussets six inches wide set into the sides of his trousers. The old man was at the back of the queue, some yards from the porridge counter, but he could see Dick was losing his temper, a frightening thing which he had witnessed twice before and did not want to see again. Harry, a small man with a flattened nose, was telling Dick that he was a bastard with a face like a pig, and a mouth as big as his belly, and he was waving his porridge ladle under Dick's nose to illustrate his point. Dick told Harry to stick his lumpy porridge up his arse and Harry hit Dick over the head with his ladle, bending it into a bow.

The kitchen-screw was knocked sideways as Dick's infuriated bulk burst through the swing doors into the kitchen and lurched towards the porridge man like a juggernaut. Harry, just as mad as the fat man but obviously decided on hit-and-run tactics, picked up his porridge tureen, now less than half full, and toppled it towards the invader, who came crashing on to the tiled floor in a sea of hot porridge.

Everybody had stopped eating and most of them were crowded round the serving-hatches yelling encouragement to the brawlers. The screws on duty at the main doors to the dining-hall, unable to get near the hatches and the doors to the kitchen because of the crush, and unable to make themselves heard above the din, were rushing up and down blowing their whistles. The old man, who had drawn level with one of the hatches when the fight started, was jammed hard against the counter unable to move, his heart thumping madly.

Dick, dripping porridge, floundered on the floor like a whale in a paddling-pool and in a terrible rage, but

Harry, seeing his man's disadvantage, bore in with a tureen of lukewarm soup and poured it over Dick's head. He followed this up with a hefty clout on Dick's head with the big wooden paddle used for stirring the soup. The din was incredible, every man in the dining-hall laughing until his sides ached and Dick bellowing like a wounded bull. Twice he made his feet and slipped back again on to the slimy floor. He gripped the edge of one of the big boilers and pulled himself up mouthing foul abuse at Harry and everybody in sight. Harry had backed into a corner and was throwing tins of uncooked fishcakes at the fat man, who didn't even seem to notice them.

The others working in the kitchen had rushed out through the back doors into the compound when the fight began, leaving the two gladiators alone in their steamy arena. And Harry, giving away at least eight stone, was cornered and frightened and making a desperate attempt to talk Dick out of murder while the crowd yelled encouragement to both of them to see it through to the finish.

Whistles were blowing everywhere in the prison and two dozen screws were barging their way through the crush to the kitchen doors. Others were rushing round the back towards the rear entrance to the kitchen. Harry was now throwing slices of bread and pats of margarine in his desperation and gasping at the same time of a truce. Dick wasn't interested. He lunged at the little man and missed, bringing the top of his head smartly against the wall. He spun round and kicked an oven over in his terrible anger and rushed after Harry, who had fled through the back door into the compound. Three screws on their way in went flying as they met Dick on his way out.

Harry was racing along by the wire with Dick, showing an amazing turn of speed for so big a man, in close pursuit, with a dozen whistle-blowing screws just behind. They rounded the corner and headed into the stretch in front of the main building just as several hundred men from the dining-hall were jostling their way outside to see the fun. Harry ran headlong into them, begging for protection, followed by Dick.

Half a dozen men went down under his weight and he struggled to his feet lashing out in all directions. The pursuing screws toppled into the mêlée and one of them got one of Dick's ham-like fists full in the face. Everybody was now trying to get out of the way except Dick, who was still trying to find Harry, and the screws, about four dozen of them by now, who were trying to subdue Dick. The chubby chief-officer hovered on the side-lines calling instructions to his men and to the prisoners to get back to the dining-hall.

Eventually Dick was subdued, an enormous porridge-and-soup-covered wretch pinned to the the ground by six screws and not caring any more about Harry. He was dragged roughly to his feet and taken off to the lock-up.

The chief went into the dining-hall with four of his

men, yelling for silence. 'You all know what happened here,' the chief said quietly. In Dartmoor and Parkhurst, Wormwood Scrubs and Pentonville he had been through this a hundred times and he knew exactly how much help he would get.

Harry was back in his kitchen and the old man, seated at his table, could hear him explaining to the kitchen-screw what happened. 'This bloke came burstin' in 'ere throwin' porridge and tins around, don't 'e? . . .' Also like Sam, Harry closed almost every remark with 'didn't I?' or 'don't 'e?' '. . . but I don't 'ave a clue who the cow was do I? 'it me over the cuntin' 'ead with the fuckin' paddle didn't 'e, so I run don't I? . . .

The old man watched the faces of the men watching the chief; vicious faces mostly, pleased but not too pleased. Too damned cowardly to put in a word for the man in the lock-up who would be on his way back to a closed prison tomorrow with loss of remission to boot. He would tell the chief himself but there was the appeal to the Home Secretary and Jane would never forgive him if anything happened to spoil his chances now. Anyway, Dick was a brute. But at least he had the decency not to feel pleased about it.

'Anybody see what happened?' asked the chief. He waited only a few seconds for a reply and barked: 'Breakfast over! Line-up outside for work in ten minutes!' The thudding in the old man's chest had stopped again. He should see a doctor about it, but they would only send him back to the Scrubs if they found anything wrong and death was better than that, he told himself.

'Lovely start to a lovely sunny day.' Frank Morgan, the man across the table from the old man, smiled ruefully. 'Yes,' he added. 'I can think of nothing better with my stale beans and sour tea than an exhibition of the noble art.'

The old man liked Frank Morgan. They had never met outside but Frank's daughter and Billy Markham had played tennis at the same club. Frank was getting out in three days after serving three years and several months of a five-year sentence. But he was finished, the old man thought. What chance has a bank manager of forty-five who robs his own bank to pay his gambling debts and his women. The man had aged greatly in the past year, too. He talked very little, and never about himself and what he would do when he got out. Frank's wife and children had not visited him for several months, yet on the first Wednesday of every month he still waited by the duty officer for a call from the gate to say his visitors had arrived. Anger welled up in the old man, not anger at Frank's wife and children, but at Frank himself. The man didn't deserve a loyal wife and family after robbing his employers and fooling around with other women. But Frank Morgan, a thief and a lecher, was getting out while he, James Hubert Markham, who had been unjustly accused of embezzlement, had another three months to serve.

Only a few men remained in the dining-hall. Sam was at his place still shovelling a hash of porridge and potato-cake into his slack mouth and spitting lumps over the table as he tried to curse and swallow at the same time. The thin man opposite, a half-dead thing with huge brown pouches under his eyes, didn't even seem to notice the lumps of porridge being spattered around him and on him. The thin man had an old two-ounce tobacco tin open on the table in front of him. The paint and lettering from the tin had been scraped off and the whole thing buffed until it gleamed and the back of a spoon had been used to press out the shapes of two hearts with an arrow through them on the lid. The inside of the tin had been divided into three compartments with slats of wood. One of the compartments held a small amount of dark tobacco and the compartment next to it a packet of Rizla cigarette papers with *Her Majesty's Prisons* printed on the cover. In the third compartment was a neat pile of matches which the thin man was splitting with a pin, his bony head bent low over the table and his eyes squinting into the light. He put his pin behind the phosphorus tip and pressed until he had pierced through to the other side. Then he pushed the pin along through the match until it fell into two halves, repeating the performance with the halves and again with the quarters until he had eight slivers of wood each with a tiny blob of phosphorus on the end.

A blob of Sam's breakfast fell into the tin but the

thin man merely picked it out with his pin, flicked it on to the floor and began work on another match. He finished three matches and took a cigarette paper from the packet, putting a pinch of the dark tobacco, kept moist by a piece of potato, into it. His thin fingers spread the half-dozen strands of tobacco evenly along the centre of the paper and rolled it into a cigarette no thicker than one of the original matches. The thin man made five of these cigarettes, putting them carefully into the compartment with the cigarette papers. He put his tin in one of the pockets of his jacket and left the table without a word.

Sam pushed his plate away with another string of oaths, wiped his mouth with the back of his sleeve and followed the thin man to the door. Others were leaving their tables and moving outside where a screw was ringing a handbell. The old man and Frank Morgan stood up together and went outside into the sunshine.

The men were assembled in their different groups along by the wire: the garden party; the farm party; the men for the wire shop where they pulled telephones to pieces all day; the men for the woodshed where they chopped bundles of firewood; four bricklayers with cement on their overalls; the men for the mattress shop where they took the wadding out of mattresses, teased it and put it back again; the coke party; the men who were helping the local vicar do his garden; the cleaners; the messengers; the hut orderlies; the spare hands; and the select few whose age and experience had taught them the best way to do nothing.

They were the barons, the book-makers, men with money and goods outside and ways and means of getting them in and out. They had tobacco, tea, milk, sugar, jam, and bread for sale at a price which a man would only pay in desperation. They did well.

Four screws patrolled up and down the lines, joking with the men, telling somebody to shut up, threatening somebody else with the lock-up. One of them, a small man from Lancashire, was checking the numbers from a big board in his hand and reminding everybody that there would be no more trouble in the dining-hall when he took charge next week.

He had a round cheerful face which could not have looked less threatening and all along the lines comments sprang from unknown origins: 'Good old Shorty' . . . 'Mind your arse on that daisy, Shorty' . . . 'Balls' . . . 'All screws are bastards' . . . 'Get on with it you twit' . . . 'How about a roll-up?' . . . 'Go and fuck yourself'. Shorty gave no sign that he had heard except to lift himself up on the balls of his feet. 'Just wate 'til I tek ower ont' thirteenth. You lot'll get summat t'be sorry abawt.'

The Governor came out from the dining-hall, where he had been questioning Harry without success on the fighting, and the noise in the lines petered away. The old man, whose nerves were on edge, was grateful for the silence. He could not stand that sort of humour; he

29

did not think it was funny at all. There was a small man in his party, a Cockney who was doing three years for altering car log-books, who was the worst offender of all. For months he had been carrying on a battle of wits with the unusually tall man standing next to him; a good-natured contest which seemed to the old man to be nothing more than a contest to see who could use the vilest language but which everybody else seemed to find particularly funny.

It followed the same pattern every day; the opening remarks from each based on the size of the other's head, legs, backside, belly, testicles, penis, feet, mouth, nose, brain, wife, wife's private parts. The short one would tell the tall one, making sure that everybody in the party could hear, that it must be cold up there. Then he would roll back on his heels, pull back his head and tap his toes up and down on the ground in satisfaction as though he had just delivered the most crushing witticism since Oscar Wilde. The tall one would reply to the effect that a shortarse couldn't possibly know as he had never been up that high to see; and he would look around in satisfaction at the rest of the party, who were invariably laughing heartily. The old man would try to shut their voices out, his nerves feeling as though they were coming out through his skin. Why didn't that damned screw give the order to march?

A late-comer was running along the front of the lines, bowing apologies to the Governor and the screws. This man, a gentle soul whose wife had died a month ago, was late every morning but nobody took any notice except the old man, who was sure he was doing it on purpose, making capital out of the fact that he had recently been bereaved. That's why we're still waiting, he thought, for that damned little Jew.

The man eased his way into the old man's line, smiling apologies all round. Another one getting out in a few days, damn his soul. A dirty little Jewish thief. He had been allowed out for the day to attend his wife's funeral and when he had come back he had gone straight to the old man's room to tell him about it. All his relatives had been there in Stoke Newington and the funeral had gone well. The Governor had given him permission to go without a prison escort as he only had a few weeks to do. The old man remembered the sadness in the man's voice as he spoke about his wife, the pain she had endured. She was better off now, he said. Damn his soul, what made him think his troubles were interesting to people who had troubles of their own. Hadn't he a wife himself and a beautiful cottage in the country and a terrible pain in his chest.

'Ohkay, moove off.' Shorty issued the command with a flourish, executing a smart right turn as the men, breaking their straight lines in the first few steps, shambled off like some sort of mad army. The farm-screw, a big man with a wide toothy grin, held open the gate as the old man led the parade out towards the open road. He stepped over the big bolt-hole cover which sat two or three inches above ground level and called: 'Watch your step', and heard the warning repeated by the man behind and on down the ranks. How many times had he said that? Four times a day, six days a week for one year, five months and twenty-eight days. And how many of the men who repeated the warning would have been happy to see somebody fall on his face and did so themselves before they could stop. The old man could feel his socks beginning to slip down into his shoes. It was not as warm as he had thought it was, either. Did that damned wind never stop for a minute?

A big white car flashed along the road in front of them, the man behind the wheel smoking a cigar. A group of schoolchildren pedalled past on their bicycles, not looking at the men. Two women with shopping baskets were standing in the road gossiping, a big brown dog sniffing along the hedgerow nearby, its nose covered with soil from rabbit holes. The old man could not understand why the old lags preferred the closed prisons where the world was out of sight.

Barker, the farm-screw, marshalled the men across the road, calling to them to get into line and to keep up. His commands made no difference to the shambles which was there on purpose. Barker knew it and so did the old man, who wished desperately the men would march properly. He could not understand what made men tread on each other's heels rather than obey, the kind of perversity encountered occasionally in the army but which here was unspoken and universal. He had seen men sent to the lock-up for doing things they did not want to do but which were part of the pointless norm which came under a dozen headings from 'To hell with the Board of Governors' to 'God rot the Lord Chief Justice'.

Barker handed the key of the tool-store to the old man and he opened the door to the smell of caked mud and oil. Another long day of spades and forks, mattocks and scythes, and billhooks and Auntie Flo's lying. The lying had been worse than anything for the old man and it went on all the time like the perversity.

There were men who told you it was fried bread for supper and positioned themselves in the dining-hall to watch your face when you discovered it was only bread-pudding. They would tell you they had read in the *Daily Express* that the Home Secretary was granting an amnesty for all prisoners over seventy and they would laugh at your attempts to get hold of a paper and then to find the story. Not good-natured laughter. The laughter, like the joke in the first place, was vindictive, part of a pattern of existence for men in bondage handed down from the days when men in loin cloths shut other men in caves.

Auntie Flo, who regarded himself as the boss of the tool-store, was the biggest liar the old man had ever met. Indeed he could not remember ever hearing the man utter a word of truth about even the most trivial matters; the time of day, the state of the weather, his name, what he had lied about a moment before. The old man wanted to kill Auntie Flo, to crush his head in with a spade and to stamp on his lying body.

Auntie Flo had a million pounds in a Swiss safe-deposit box, a Rolls, a Bentley, a Daimler and any other car mentioned in earshot. He had been married eight times to wealthy women and he kept two well-known film actresses in flats near Park Lane. He had a yacht berthed at Cannes; three hundred and sixty-five suits; a controlling interest in I.C.I.; no criminal record because he was really a government agent in here to trap 'Mr. Big'; a system for beating the bank at Monte Carlo which had been tried with such success that de Gaulle had had to lend money to the Casino to put it back on its feet; a photographic memory, a judo black belt, a fear of nothing, a V.C., Purple Heart, Croix de Guerre, a bald yellow head and the most highly polished shoes in the prison. He was called Auntie Flo because he teetered and lied in a high-pitched, auntyish voice.

The men pushed their way up to the counter, anxious to collect their tools and begin their daily search for a skive, a quiet corner of some forgotten field where they could rest in peace. Auntie Flo greeted the first man at the counter: 'Good evening. You're Smith and you want a spade.' The man, who had been through this routine a hundred times before, was called Jenkins and he always had a fork. The old man handed him his fork and the man went off glowering back at Auntie Flo, who was telling the next man that the rakes had woodworm and would he take a tractor instead. The old man looked at the top of Auntie Flo's head and imagined what he could do to it with a spade. Could the man never give a straight answer to anything? Was he mad, or what?

Auntie Flo was telling a newcomer how to get to the greenhouses, directing him away from them at an angle of one hundred and eighty degrees. The newcomer went off with a Dutch hoe because Auntie Flo had told him that nobody went off to the greenhouse without one and he was persuading two men who wanted lettuce trays that the whole crop had been taken by blight during the night and that Barker wanted them to take two hatchets and go to the woodshed. Barker came in to discover the reason for the hold-up and Auntie Flo told the farm-screw he was having trouble with two men who wanted hatchets when they should be taking lettuce trays. The two men started to argue but Barker pushed them towards the door and told Auntie Flo to get on with it and watch his step.

But Auntie Flo never watched his step. He had been beaten more than any other man in the prison to no purpose at all. Auntie Flo would die a violent death telling the Governor he had been murdered by a man in a purple suit wielding a billhook and answering to the name of Bonaparte.

The other man in the tool-store hardly spoke at all and if he did it was nearly always to say something nice about somebody or something. He had been a postman until he stole a registered letter one day and he had only served a few months of a three-year sentence which he said he deserved as just punishment for his diabolical crime.

Another Judge with a conveyor-belt mind had meted out abuse of trust, public servant, callous disregard for the feelings of others and the ex-postman had agreed with every word. His wife had run away with another man shortly after his conviction, which was reasonable, too. His son had sold his furniture and gambled the money at Romford dogs and who could blame him? It seemed to the old man that no amount of abuse and degradation could stir up anger or bitterness in the postman.

The old man wanted to kill the postman, too. He also wanted the postman to escape and kill his wife and son like any red-blooded man would. God, were there no normal men in this terrible place; men who liked refined women and good food, who were members of the bridge club and played golf at Wentworth and knew the head waiter at Simpson's. There was George at the admin. block, of course. George was an Old Etonian and, like himself, a victim of circumstance. He would go and check that the potted plants in the admin. block were all right for water.

It was warm now in spite of the wind. Several men in a nearby carrot field had stripped off their shirts. The sun would soon redden their white skin. The old man strolled slowly, massaging his right thigh with his hand. The stiffness seemed to be moving up past his hip towards his waist and downwards towards his knee.

CHAPTER 3

George, the Old Etonian, considered himself a cut above just about everything on two feet, so much so that there were less than half a dozen people in the entire establishment he would even be seen talking to. There was nothing subtle or underlying about his arrogance, either. He looked as haughty as a Siamese cat and his disposition was roughly similar.

The old man had often wondered how George had managed to escape physical injury during more than five years behind prison walls, but the odd fact was the Old Etonian was held in high regard by most of the men he shunned. Not awe, for men in captivity reserve their awe for men who escape in a spectacular manner, or who steal vast sums of money or kill policemen. It was not that they felt inferior to him, either. A man who bears himself staunchly under injustice, knows everything worth knowing, loves all humankind except policemen, prison officers, barons, informers, workmen, Jews, Catholics, people who don't smoke, and teenagers, is inferior to nobody. It was probably the fact that George asked for nothing and appeared to have everything.

He had a system for acquiring things which by-passed the barons, to their chagrin, and which nobody had been able to unravel. The old man had never asked George where he got his tins of Nescafé or his tailor-made cigarettes because he knew in the first place that George would not tell him and also that it would probably wreck the delicate balance of their friendship. The old man was under no illusions about their relationship. He knew that George found his company just about acceptable, the closest thing to a pretender to near-equality available while the village vicar was in Germany on holiday. But George did not tell lies; in fact, he rarely told anything. He provided warm, sweet coffee and the occasional biscuit, and he was prepared in a cold-blooded way to discuss the theatre or the Stock Exchange without one having to be a cousin of Sir Laurence Olivier or once having bought tin at threepence in the morning and sold it for fifteen shillings in the afternoon.

The old man invariably did most of the talking,

always keeping the topic of conversation general. There had once been an occasion early in his friendship with George, when in a particularly dejected moment, he had begun to discuss his case and then his wife and son. George had not let him finish; in fact he had told him very abruptly that if he wanted to air his troubles he could do so elsewhere. The old man had at first felt anger and then sheer misery and had been determined to go nowhere near George again. But the following day George had invited him for a cup of coffee as though nothing had happened and the old man had accepted. Honest friends, even without warmth, were hard to find.

The old man tapped on the window of the cubbyhole where George made tea for the Governor and his staff. There was a complicated rigmarole attached to having coffee with George which involved checking the whereabouts of everybody in the building, organising an alarm system and then thinking up a reason why the old man was there in the first place. The alarm system was usually an incredibly battered and bent old lag who swept the floors of the admin. block and who, for a cigarette, would whistle 'Rule, Britannia!' if authority looked like approaching the cubbyhole, which was practically never.

After every visit, George reminded the old man to think up a good reason for his journey before coming to the admin. block but the old man's imagination was never up to it. As he left the tool-store he invariably told himself that just checking the potted plants for water was good enough but by the time he got there he knew it would not do, particularly as the potted plants were nothing to do with the tool-shed anyway.

The few minutes it took George to lay on his precautions always had the old man in a fever of anxiety, not because he was afraid of the consequences of being caught, but because a man of seventy-five feels foolish when he is caught standing in a rhododendron bush outside a window like a schoolboy stealing apples. He began to wonder now if the whole silly carry-on was worth a cup of coffee and a chat with a man who didn't even like him.

George had left the cubby-hole and was no doubt making his haughty way round the offices, making sure that the occupants were where they should be, before giving the old lag his cigarette and reminding him not to go to sleep on his broom. A figure swept past the open doorway to the cubby-hole in the corridor beyond and the old man ducked instinctively into his bush to straighten up immediately, feeling more foolish than ever. To be caught standing in the bush was one thing; to be caught squatting in it like a thief was another. He would count to ten and if George was not back by then he would leave, and to hell with his coffee.

He got to nine the second time around before George opened the little window and told him it was all clear in the hall but he had better come round quickly. The old man could feel his heart thumping with the excitement as he closed the door quietly after him and sat down on the chair by the little deal table.

'It's nearly ready,' said George, not looking at the old man. 'If anybody comes, you're here to collect a trowel I borrowed.'

The cubby-hole was about six feet square with a gas ring on a small cupboard in one corner, the small deal table, and two folding chairs. From the tiny window there was a fine view of open fields dotted with farmhouses. Men were working in the fields with tractors and horses, free men who would go to lunch when they were hungry or perhaps take a stroll down to the village pub for a pint of beer and some bread and cheese.

The old man pictured himself with them in the public bar, the beer in cool, pewter tankards moist with condensation on the outside, the bread still warm from the oven and crisp. All those years in the City getting richer and cultivating men who had never earned a penny by the sweat of their brows. They were not his kind of people, the grafters, the wheelers and dealers in pieces of paper. There was more to life than a three-litre Rover and a mock-Tudor home in the stockbroker belt.

Outside there was a life, basic God-fearing life, with salary commensurate with ability and no daggers in the back. Humility descended on the old man more often as time went along, pushing him down to greater extremes of self-effacement. In these moods he silently promised God a life of service to others, unswerving kindness to man and beast. If only God would pull him through this time of trial unharmed. There were still some years of usefulness in him, years to be spent quietly in the country with his wife and friends, helping those less fortunate, bottling jams and fruits for motherless children, visiting those in hospital.

The men in the distance were breaking off for morning tea and the old man could see a buxom woman walking towards them from a farmhouse with a huge enamel jug in her hand. Sweating, cursing farm-labourers knocking off five minutes early and making dirty jokes about the fat woman with the tea-jug. Beer-sodden men who beat their wives and let their children run shabby in the fields, men whining about the greed and meanness of the farmer while they stole his vegetables and eggs and chickens and fell behind with their rent. Ordinary men with the minimum of honesty and maximum of sour grapes displayed on a picture post-card for another man with only hope, and that an uncertain thing.

The sun was warm through the window and George opened it a little to clear the steam from the kettle. He measured the coffee carefully into two cups, filled them with water and poured a little sweetened milk from a tin into each. 'There you are, James. We haven't much time this morning, I have to see the welfare officer before lunch.' He pencilled in a clue in his *Daily Telegraph* crossword puzzle while he stirred his coffee with his other hand. The old man wished George would ask him to help.

The old man desperately wanted to tell somebody about the pain in his chest. No, he wanted somebody to tell him it was nothing but indigestion or a natural discomfort of advancing years. And no again, because the old man did not want it to be nothing, or even something as uncomplicated as indigestion.

Was he not throwing himself on the mercy of the Home Secretary and the Archbishop of Canterbury as an old sick man? But where to draw a fine line between illness and health? Something non-malignant, not too painful. Tuberculosis, perhaps. That was not dangerous these days and it gave you the appearance of chronic illness without too much pain. But they might let him out and send him to a sanitorium or even keep him in here longer until he was cured.

Diabetes? No, there were the injections and the old man had always been afraid of the needle. There was a man who slept down the corridor from him who had diabetes, a half-dead thing who seemed to have no flesh at all on his bones. The old man, before he could stop himself, had imagined the needle going into this man, through white, crinkly skin and jarring hard against the bone. He had imagined the needle snapping off beneath the skin and the thought had set his teeth on edge even though he had lost the last of them twenty years before. No, not diabetes.

There were books he had read in which people had unnamed, non-fatal illnesses which seemed in no way to detract from their enjoyment of life and at the same time endowed the sufferer with a certain interest. But this was not like that. This was pain, deep-rooted pain like a hand inside his chest squeezing his innards with all its might. Then there were the dizzy spells when he stooped or straightened suddenly, and the blackness which seemed to sweep upwards over his eyes as if he were being filled from below with dark liquid which one day would reach his brain and he would die.

He had tried to tell Bert about it but Bert had not understood. It was so difficult to explain, especially to someone who was not very good at understanding in the first place and the old man had not mentioned it again. Bert had said what the old man wanted him to say; that it was nothing serious and not to go near prison doctors because they were all bastards who amputated at the drop of a hat and who were too dim to get a job outside, which was why they were what they were, bastards. The old man wanted assurance and for a while he had been satisfied. But now he wanted assurance from a higher authority, someone who would consider before he spoke and would then repeat what Bert had said without the unnecessary condemnation of the prison medical service.

George had put down his pencil and was looking at him with that odd, completely dispassionate look on his face. The old man could hear his heart beating faster.

To hell with it, he was going to ask George for his advice even if he was in for another snub. The old man cleared his throat.

'There's something I've been meaning to speak to you about.' He had tried to make it by-the-by and it had come out rehearsed . . . to speak to you about . . . about which I have been meaning . . . by the way, George. What a damn silly way to begin a conversation.

George hadn't batted an eyelid or even twitched a muscle on his long, haughty face. Just look at the bastard, he can see right through me. The old man cleared his throat again. 'It's this pain, George.' Christ almighty, he had done it. He'd gone and told George it was a personal problem in his first breath when he had made such careful plans to make it hypothetical. But George still had not changed his expression. A wave of panic swept over the old man, a panic to get it over with, to ask his question and be done with it.

'I don't know what to do about it you see,' he said, looking at the floor in front of him now, not daring to look George in the face. 'It's worse in the morning just after I get up. . . .' The old man blundered on, furious with himself for the inadequate way he was describing his symptoms but not daring to pause to search in his mind for a better word or a better description. 'It begins low down in my chest and builds up. . . .' No it doesn't, you fool, it comes across from left to right. Never mind, he had described the pain itself fairly well and that was what really mattered. 'Then there are these dizzy spells as if my head is spinning round and my eyes seem to go black.'

That wasn't right, his eyes didn't go black. 'Not exactly black, George, but a sort of greyness.' Blindness. That would not be too bad. He could sit quietly in his big arm-chair listening to the radio or Jane could read to him and on sunny days they could go for a walk with their dog. They couldn't keep a blind man in jail. Or would they? There had been a blind man at the Scrubs, he seemed to remember somebody telling him. But they would probably let him out for treatment and that would be almost as good as being. . . .

George cut into his thoughts, his flat drawling voice making the old man jump slightly. 'I don't really see where the problem lies at all,' he said. 'Go and ask the prison doctor, that's what he's there for.'

The old man felt as though he had been struck in the face. He stared at the floor feeling the anger bubble up inside him, his hands gripping the arms of his chair. 'Is that all you can bloody well suggest?' The words were almost whispered but he knew that his next would be a scream. 'Christ, as if I don't know what prison doctors are there for. They're there to fuck you up, to make sure if there's nothing wrong with you there bloody soon will be.' The old man was gasping for breath, very nearly in tears. He wanted to put his boot in the Old Etonian's long face; number three on his I-would-like-to-murder list for the morning.

Humility disappeared as humility will when it is put

46

on like a plastic raincoat to ward off a shower of the miseries. The old man spluttered on: 'Don't tell me what to do, you bloody phoney bastard crook. There's nothing wrong with me, and you damn well know it, except you're too bloody pompous to say a kind word about anybody or anything . . . you can't even. . . .'

'I have a daughter . . .' George had not altered the expression on his face and his voice had the same flat, haughty tone. The old man, white with anger, stopped spluttering. It was not the fact that George had spoken that shocked him into silence but the realisation that the man had told him something about his private life for the first time in countless conversations. 'She has cancer. She's only eighteen,' said George. 'She's going to be dead within a month. That's why I have to see the welfare officer; they're sending me back to Parkhurst. They are afraid I will try to escape.'

The old man blinked at his companion, hardly able to believe the position in which he suddenly found himself and, most appalling of all, having to struggle to feel sorry for either George or his daughter.

'Sorry,' he said. To hell with it why should he be sorry for some blasted girl he'd never met. Her father was a crook, wasn't he? 'Dreadfully sorry,' he said, trying to make himself smaller in the hard wooden chair. Christ, hadn't he enough to be sorry about without somebody else's sick brat? What right had this man to burden him with his family troubles when he had this crippling pain in his chest and his wife and friend were having a good time while he was locked away and his daughter-in-law had never been to visit him? 'What a terrible thing,' he said. What did this man care about his daughter? He was a thief. Parkhurst! Christ, they sent the really bad ones there, didn't they. If he was that fond of his daughter why didn't he stay with her instead of stealing money and running around with a lot of West End tarts? That's what he'd done, more than likely.

The old man stood up suddenly, gripping the edge of the chair to steady himself. 'You'd better not be late for your appointment,' he said, edging towards the door. 'I hope things will be better soon.' He backed out through the door and almost ran out into the sunshine.

Red Barrel stepped down the road with his hands clasped behind his back like Prince Philip. The jacket of his prison overalls flapped in the breeze and his hobnail boots made an echoing sound through the tarmac of the road. He walked with his head down but his eyes glanced from side to side repeatedly. A man strolling in the spring sunshine. A nervous man.

Red Barrel did not know that George's daughter was dying and if he had it is doubtful that he would have cared. He knew there was an old man hoping to get out because he was ill, but as he did not think about that either he did not call the old man a bloody fool, or worse. Red Barrel did not have problems, or if he did, he did not recognise them as such. There were situations, obstacles, poxy binds, drags. If there had ever been a time when Red Barrel saw a clear road ahead he could not remember it. He was thirty-five years old and into those years he had crammed a dozen lifetimes of conniving.

But not now. This was straightforward. Three hundred yards down this road was a public house. the 'Red Fox', where they sold draught bitter by the pint. And squeezed tightly in the palm of Red Barrel's right hand was a half-crown which had cost him an ounce of tobacco.

He could almost feel the cool glass on the inside of his big lower lip and the tickle of the froth as it edged up his upper lip and almost into his nose. In his mind he bit the beer from the glass in large chunks and felt the chunks drop into his stomach with a thud of exquisite satisfaction. Just one pint, because there would be no time for any more even if he had the money. And one was all he wanted. Just one pint of Watney's and they could take him back to pay the bill.

Red Barrel quickened his step, flicking his eyes from side to side. A farmworker on a bicycle pedalled past him going in the opposite direction and called 'good morning'. Red Barrel called 'good morning' back and the sound of his own voice startled him. The bend in the road was fifty yards ahead. Once round the bend he would be able to see the pub, a hundred yards or so along on the left.

Out of the corner of his left eye he could see a grey-haired figure walking from the direction of the admin. block towards the main gate and in the distance a screw watching over a gang of men working in a field. To his right, the diamond mesh separated him from the prison proper. Behind the mesh and just ahead of him was the prison officers' club.

This was it, thought Red Barrel, clasping tighter to his half-crown. Walk slower, you silly cow. He slowed his pace slightly and kept his eyes on the ground in front of him. He could hear voices in the club and laughter. Christ, that bad bastard Herbert was in there. If one of them was near the window that would be the end of it.

He walked past the club, not daring to look towards it, and round the bend in the road. There it was, the 'Red Fox'. He could see the sign jutting out over the road just as he remembered it from the prison bus when they had brought him here nine months ago. He fought to stop himself from running but even so he could see from the hedgerows he was moving fast.

Ninety yards, eighty yards, seventy yards, sixty yards. . . . A whistle sounded in the distance to his left and Red Barrel broke into a run. He looked to his left as he ran and he could see the screw from the field, four hundred yards or so away, running towards the road, waving his arms. Another whistle, from behind him this time and very faint. And another from the same direction.

Red Barrel pounded across the gravel forecourt of the

pub and stopped outside the glass doors of the public bar. No, not the public. They would look there first. Stop gasping, you cow. The barman'll spot you a mile off. He walked round the corner of the building and back again to the door marked 'saloon', straightened his jacket and walked in.

The feel of the swing door under his hand and the sweet smell of beer that hit his nostrils with gentle force brought bubbles of saliva to his lips. There they were: the shiny black handles of the pumps, the rows of carefully dusted bottles, the gleaming bar pitted by a million pint glasses thumped down in an unspoken demand for more ale. The longing, clutching at Red Barrel's stomach like an iron hand, made him want to moan out loud.

He eased the half-crown from his sweating palm and dropped it on to the bar. A group of men at a table in the corner were looking at him. Damn their bloody eyes, the miserable bastards. But the Red Barrel looked away from them. Where the hell was the barman? Christ, was that a whistle? It sounded close. Barman, barman. He wanted to shout. He wanted to jump over the bar and pull a pint for himself and pour it into his face. That was a whistle all right, and another, and another.

The men at the corner table were still looking at him, he could tell. He could feel their eyes taking in every inch of him from his prison boots to the top of his prison haircut. Barman, barman.

'Barman!'

He felt the men in the corner start at his shout which sounded hoarse and unreal in his own ears. He picked up the half-crown and smacked it down on the bar.

'Barman!'

The barman came out of the doorway behind the bar, a little man in a soiled white jacket and as surly-looking as anything Red Barrel had seen in a lifetime of surly faces. The miserable, cringing little runt. 'Pint of best, please.' The 'please' came hard, the miserable little shithouse. But the man was looking at him too hard. 'Christ, I'm thirsty.' The barman looked towards the men in the corner and back at Red Barrel, who was now leaning over the bar towards him. 'A pint of best bitter. I'm thirsty.' Thirsty! They didn't know, these bastards. How could these bastards know.

The barman was pulling at the pump in front of him, slowly. Too much froth. Damn you you stupid little cow, too much froth. Another whistle, very close. The barman had stopped pulling and was looking at Red Barrel, at his face and at his overalls and his striped shirt and his stringy tie. A car ran into the forecourt and skidded to a halt on the gravel and several doors slammed at once. A whistle sounded immediately outside and then another.

Somebody shouted: 'Get round the back . . . !' Red Barrel heard feet running on the gravel and through the partition he saw Herbert, big, red-faced Herbert, burst in through the swing doors to the public bar.

Herbert saw Red Barrel almost instantaneously and wheeled round and back out through the doors, blowing the whistle clasped between his teeth.

Herbert's voice, a thick, West Country voice, was shouting that the quarry was in the saloon, large as life; gleefully, like a boy who has cornered a rabbit. Red Barrel heard feet rushing about on the gravel outside the door and the crunching of tyres on the gravel and more doors slamming as a second car arrived. He could see shadows through the glass door and he swung round on the barman with a roar which sent the little man scuttling backwards into the shelves of bottles.

Red Barrel swung himself over the bar, rapping his shin against a wooden crate of empties on the floor as he landed. He hardly noticed the pain. The barman had dropped the glass and fled out through the door behind the bar while the customers at the corner table were standing in nervous silence; fear, amusement and disgust all mixed up on their faces. They moved farther back into the corner as the door crashed open and six screws, with Herbert in the lead, rushed in.

Red Barrel had a pint glass under the spout of the pump and was pulling at the shiny black pump handle jerkily. He could hear the beer spitting into the glass but he kept his eyes on Herbert's face as the screws moved carefully towards him across the few feet of open floor between the door and the bar. Herbert was grinning. The miserable, soulless bastard.

They came at him in a lump of blue serge before he

knew what was happening. Herbert was over the bar head first and grasped him by the neck, pulling him to the ground. Somebody had him by the legs and somebody else was on top of him, pulling his head back by the hair. Herbert's face was pressed against his own, his huge, false teeth bared in a grin which could have been amusement or effort. His breath smelled of stale beer.

The glass still clutched in Red Barrel's hand was half full of beer and Herbert held the wrist of the hand holding the glass. Red Barrel, a terrible rage in him, pulled the glass towards his face, seeing the knuckles of Herbert's hand go white as he fought to push the glass away. 'No beer for the likes of you, laddie. No beer for cons, laddie.' But Red Barrel was winning. He could almost taste it. He exerted every ounce of his strength and saw Herbert's arm bending under the strain and he laughed to himself as he heard Herbert's grunt of effort. Then Herbert let go.

The beer slashed into his face and eyes and up his nose. His own fist brought the heavy glass smashing into his own face. It dug into the bridge of his nose and he held it there, sucking at emptiness. His tongue reached out around his mouth for a taste of beer, just one goddam lousy taste of beer. Just one. Please, just a taste.

Blood ran into his mouth, and tears. Beer soaked the front of his shirt and Red Barrel could see beer on the floor a few inches from his broken nose. He laid his head on the wet floor and wept. They could have let him drink it, the miserable bastards. But no, that wasn't in the rules. It was not part of the game to let a man throw away a year of his life for a pint of best bitter and let him have the bitter as well.

They bundled him into the back seat of one of the cars. Herbert sat on one side and a screw Red Barrel couldn't remember having seen before, a younger man, on the other.

Herbert nudged Red Barrel with his elbow and grinned. 'No beer for cons, laddie. I told you.' He chuckled and rubbed his hands. 'No, laddie. It's back to Parkhurst for you, laddie, and no mistake.' The younger screw told Herbert to shut up but Herbert laughed. 'You'll meet scabs like this again, old son. When you get dry behind the ears.' He put his head back and laughed and smacked his knee.

The vultures are out, thought Red Barrel, as the car drew in through the prison gate. Look at them, the nosy pigs. There's that soft old bastard whose wife's written to the Home Secretary. The stupid old bitch.

The farm-party was held up at the gate while the car drove through and the old man knew something was going on because the Governor and the chief officer were there watching and looking worried. He knew Red Barrel was in the car because everybody said so. But he did not know how they knew. And he had no time to think about it because Taffy was observing.

Taffy had a big, red, smiling face and a huge stomach and he was doing five for setting fire to a house he said was his own in Pontlottyn. Taffy was an observer. He observed everything and commented on it: the rising of the moon, the going down of the sun; over and over again. There were men in here who wanted to cripple Taffy because he observed out loud on dangerous topics like the exchange of tobacco. But Taffy was too big and strong.

On the way over from the farm the old man had been trying to shut out Taffy's observing from one ear and the terrible pleadings of an alcoholic from the other. He did not want to think about dying girls and alcoholics and he did not want to know that a red bus could be seen proceeding east in the distance.

The alcoholic, a youngish man with grey hair, was asking for the tobacco he had paid for. The man he was asking, a pleasant-looking man, was explaining that demand was vastly exceeding supply and that he, as a mere carrier for the baron, could be held in no way responsible for this terrible lapse in delivery.

Taffy had seen the welfare officer with his coat unbuttoned, which was something well and truly out of the ordinary. Yes indeed. The welfare officer with his coat unbuttoned was something to be remarked upon.

No, wretched alcoholic, you cannot have the contents of our tobacco tin because that is reserved for another customer with prior claims. A customer, in fact, who is prepared to pay not twice, but three times. The name of the baron? Are you mad? With observers like Taffy around? Christ! What next!

A car full of screws and an unidentified, blood-stained man to be sure. Proceeding in the direction of the lock-up. Now that was something out of the ordinary. My, my. . . . Oh no, desperate alcoholic with the pain of longing burning at your insides, there is no question here of tobacco on credit. Price, ha ha, is determined by demand.

A blood-stained man and no question about it. To be sure. No question about it. . . . Out of the question, old chap. Threats, is it? We had better forget that, old chap. Our face wouldn't look too good stove in. Nothing to do with me, mind you. Tell you what, see me after lunch and we'll see about a few roll-ups in advance. You're sure your wife sent the money?

The farm-screw, who was sweating and in an ill humour, opened the gate and the old man led the way through. He called 'Watch your step' as he passed over the bolt-hole.

CHAPTER 4

Beginning at the end of the year, cornflakes would be served twice a week to inmates of Her Majesty's Prisons. The days on which the cornflakes would replace the usual porridge would be left to the discretion of the Governors, who would also have the authority to decide in what manner the cornflakes were served.

These facts were contained in a well-fingered cutting from one of the responsible daily newspapers which had been handed down the queue from the serving-hatches and had now reached the old man, who had just heard for the seventh time in a few minutes how the screws had caught up with Red Barrel as he was about to put a pint of bitter to his lips. The poor bastard, one of the tellers had explained, had not even had a chance to get a drop of the beer down his gullet and was now in solitary awaiting shipment back to Parkhurst, the poor bastard.

It was amazing, thought the old man, how the facts were known already when Red Barrel had only been taken into custody a few minutes before. The versions differed only on the point of the measure of beer involved and on whether Red Barrel was a poor bastard with guts or a drunken bastard without sense, or a cunning bastard who owed so much tobacco he had engineered the whole thing to avoid paying it back. The arguments on these points had been increasing in heat when the cutting about the cornflakes made its way down the lunch queue and cast Red Barrel adrift in his solitary cell beside the mattress shop.

Cornflakes? Christ almighty! Cornflakes? Bugger me! Cornflakes? Told the bastard, didn't I? The word danced in the air, jumped over the tables, swung from the electric lights, ricocheted off the walls, buzzed across the floor until the old man felt his head was going to burst.

Cornflakes, cornflakes, cornflakes, cornflakes . . . every man said it once, then again and again and again, with question marks, exclamation marks, asterisks. Cornflakes by Christ, by Jesus, by hell, by heck; cornflakes be buggered and be a dozen things. Then the opinions, a thousand million opinions on cornflakes: where they came from and where they were going and why; what they were made of and what they were not made of and ought to be; that they were made in Hong Kong from infected wheat especially for us poor bastards; that they were cheaper to produce than porridge which was not really porridge but pig meal; that the Board of Governors owned a cornflakes factory; that cornflakes contained nil vitamins and nil protein and would be eaten with nil milk and nil sugar.

You couldn't believe a damned thing you read in the newspapers because the Governor had never mentioned cornflakes, the deputy-Governor had never mentioned cornflakes, the chief officer had never mentioned cornflakes, the cookhouse-screw had never mentioned cornflakes, and if there was a man in the prison who would know about cornflakes it would be the cookhouse-screw because he would have to supervise the distribution of the cornflakes.

But it was there in black and white: beginning at the end of the year cornflakes would be served. . . . You could not argue with facts. Cornflakes, cornflakes, cornflakes. . . . The queue shuffled past the serving-hatches and the word became an all-over hum as it was taken quietly and loudly, knowingly and in surprise, to the tables.

'Just how many manners are there in which you can serve you know what,' said Frank Morgan as the old man sat down gingerly with his tray. Thank God for a human being. He felt better. Jane and Tom would be here in an hour and a half and he did not have to go to work this afternoon. He would be able to pick up his *Daily Telegraph* after lunch and read it on his bed until they arrived.

The fishcake had sharp bones in it, the potatoes were not cooked through and the custard was thin and watery. To help it down, the little diabetic on the table behind leaned over to remind all that he had to see the doctor tomorrow to have his water tested. But the old man felt nearly cheerful. He was determined to think of nothing, to close his mind to everything so as not to spoil it. He would save the *Daily Telegraph* until this evening.

The aluminium trays slotted neatly into each other, their clatter softened by the thin film of food left on each after the men had scraped their leavings into a big bin. The piles rose neatly as the old man watched, leaning slightly where a few too many had been added to a pile, but still regular and pleasing to look at. Then Sam, his unshaven face spattered with grease and custard and pieces of potato, pushed his tray on top of one of the piles without bothering, as usual, to scrape it clean.

It rested out of true and the man behind put his tray on top of it without putting Sam's tray straight. The man behind did the same and the next man and the next, until the pile tilted awkwardly. The old man and Frank Morgan looked at each other and then back at the trays, which looked as though they were actually swaying.

Another man put his tray on top of the faulty pile

and another, and the pile swayed over into the next one knocking it against the next one and that against the next. In slow motion the mountain of aluminium, perched high on a steel table, crashed to the floor with a crack like thunder. The old man had been ready for it but he jumped all the same. So did Frank Morgan but the other half-dozen or so men who were left in the dining-hall, who had not seen what was about to happen, leapt to their feet as if they had been stung.

Harry, the porridge man, burst through the swing doors from the kitchen, crouched low and ready to defend himself and offering abuse to God and everybody as he came. The number one kitchen-screw was close behind with a broom in his hands and alarm on his face.

Trays had skidded across the polished floor scattering greasy food everywhere. The waste-bin had been knocked over in the crash sending a stream of green-pea soup, fishcake, potato, cabbage, college pudding and custard between the tables. The kitchen-screw lowered his broom from the attack position, looked carefully at the diners to make sure that nobody was laughing and then at Harry, who was, uncontrollably.

'Clean it up,' ordered the screw, prodding his broom in Harry's direction.

'Who?' Harry had stopped laughing and was spluttering in disbelief. 'Not me, sir. Bollocks to that, sir. Told the bastards to be careful, didn't I? Told the sloppy cows to put the trays straight, didn't I?'

The screw advanced a step on the porridge man.

'Clean it up or we'll go and see the Governor.' Harry seemed on the point of protesting some more, but changed his mind and stalked into the kitchen. 'Outside, the rest of you,' ordered the screw, who had been in the prison service for thirty years and had learned a long time ago that questions were useless. Besides, he had watched the fight at breakfast time and knew who had started it. The evil little sod would have been back in Dartmoor by now except for the fact that he made edible porridge. It was hard enough to find a man who didn't piss in it.

The screw went back to the kitchen and Frank Morgan and the old man walked together into the compound and began their usual silent lunch-time stroll three times around the block. The starers had already lined themselves up on their bench by the bowling-green from where they could see three-quarters of the promenade. Four pairs of eyes without faces or figures.

These men were not observers like Taffy. They watched without purpose or interest and made no comment on what they saw. There was no intensity in their stares. Their eyes, the only features by which the old man could recognise them, followed a walker as if attracted to him magnetically, abandoning him for another when a movement of the head would be necessary to follow further.

The old man had never seen these men read a book or a newspaper. He had often wondered if in them he had discovered the ultimate in sloth. They used their legs and arms and mouths for walking, working, and eating which were all either essential for survival or demanded by the authorities. But in their leisure moments when the choice was theirs they activated the one set of muscles which, in the whole of their bodies, probably required the least effort. There was an unclean stillness about the four men.

Frank Morgan did only one lap of the compound and left the old man to see if there was any mail for either of them. There would be no mail for the old man today because his wife and friend were coming, and there would be none for Frank because his wife and children had stopped writing. Frank would not come back because he would be afraid the pain would show in his face. He would go to his room, lie on his bed and try not to think.

At visiting-time he would assemble with the others outside the duty-screw's office. One by one, names would be called until there was only Frank left and it would not matter if the pain showed. The old man knew that Frank Morgan loved his wife and children, as most men do when they no longer have them. Right now he himself loved his wife and even the daughter-in-law who would not visit him.

The bell rang for the men to assemble in front of the dining-hall to be marched back to work. The old man watched them shuffle into ragged lines and he saw the little Jew arrive late, bowing apologies all round. He watched them all march off out of step. The big gates swung open, the men tramped across the road towards the farm and the gates closed with a clank and a rattling. This was the beginning of the best hour of the month, when only the men expecting visitors and the people who worked there remained in the main compound. And these men did not want to talk.

It was an hour of anticipation, a particularly pleasant hour, thought the old man, for someone who was sure that what he was expecting would arrive. The pain in his chest had gone altogether and the muscles in his leg felt freer. The sun was warm. The wind had dropped, too. A screw from the clothing-store, a big, friendly man, smiled as he passed on his way back to work.

Jane and Tom would just be finishing lunch. What if they already had news from the Home Secretary! They could have heard something since Jane's last letter. The old man pulled his shoulders back and stepped out round the compound at a brisker pace. He smiled up at the sky and thought of funny things.

God, but they told some damned funny stories, some of these old lags. If only he had a tape recorder so that Jane and Tom could hear them properly. They always sounded so flat when he tried to retell them.

That Bert! What a character. He had been in every nick in the country, according to him, and he had been the terror of them all. It was the telling of the stories that counted, of course. And the language. That was one of the drawbacks, having to tone down the language for Jane's benefit.

There was that chap who had escaped from Strangeways and had gone to the Isle of Man where he had dyed his hair purple. God, Bert had him in stitches with that one. Purple, for God's sake. He had dyed his hair purple because he thought making himself conspicuous was the best sort of camouflage. The first policeman that saw him arrested him. The old man chuckled out loud, Probably not true, but what an imagination that Bert had.

Then there was that chap in solitary in Dartmoor who dug a tunnel and was caught by the screws as he was about to remove the last stone to freedom. 'Oh, God,' the man had said. But it was the way Bert told the story that nearly made you die laughing. How about that chap who wouldn't wash and they locked him in a laundry-skip and left him in the middle of the football pitch all night. February, too, and snowing like hell. 'Stiff as a board and nearly dead,' Bert had told him. God, but that had been funny. The old man chuckled to himself now at Bert's stories and a dozen other stories he had heard from men like Bert.

Men who made fun of pain so long as it was not their own. The old man stopped chuckling and he stopped remembering stories. Jane would bring him a cigar and chicken sandwiches and some cakes made with fresh cream. You were not allowed to have sandwiches in the visiting-room, only biscuits and cakes, but Jane made the sandwiches so small and thin they looked like biscuits. Jane and Tom would be full of news, probably, and he would be too excited to eat much.

Men like Bert had their own peculiar code of morals, though. They never squealed on each other and they would not tolerate offences against children. They did terrible things, Bert had said, to men who were in prison for molesting or mistreating children. One man in Parkhurst had had to spend the whole of his five-year sentence in solitary because every time they let him associate with the other prisoners he had been brutally beaten. The man had molested a little girl, Bert had said. The bastard ought to have been castrated, Bert had said. Killing would have been too good for the poxy cow, Bert had said.

Bert had said. The old man tried to push Bert out of his mind and the frightening violence which went hand-in-hand with everything Bert said and did.

Who was this man who molested little girls? Was he a sick man? And if he was, who cared? Bert didn't care and the men who murdered grandmothers, fathers, aunts, uncles didn't care because they knew where decency ended and the unspecified age at which rape or attempted rape is permissible.

The Berts with their unassailable ethics had read in a lying newspaper that Detective Chief Superintendent Thingummy (and don't we all know that he lies to his mother?) had stated on oath at —shire Assizes that Cassius O'Connor Blumberg, an Irish Jew with coloured blood (and wouldn't you just know it, the bastard), had brutally and without feeling attempted to interfere with a young girl.

What could be plainer? Say no more. Despatch Cassius O'Connor Blumberg to one of H.M. Prisons where we rapists who know where to draw the line, we murderers, blackmailers, drug pedlars and such will beat the living daylights out of him at every opportunity until twisted, vicious, inhuman, sick Mr Blumberg takes his own worthless life or is carried off in a strait-jacket to Broadmoor, which is where he belongs and is much too good for him. If there is one thing we Berts cannot stand it is these slimy Cassius O'Connor Blumbergs trying to wriggle out from under the brilliant and impartial cross-examination of you, Chief Superintendent Thingummys, with your undoubted fairness when it comes to this sort of thing.

The old man was struggling again. Dammit, why couldn't you turn your mind off like a water tap when you have done with it? Happiness was no longer an easy state of mind. It was something you had to fight for every minute of the day because relax for a moment and you would think of something bad. It was physical too. You had to take a grip on yourself and literally haul your body into a state of well-being. The whole thing was tiring, especially for a man of nearly eighty.

The old man quickened his pace still more, glancing sharply from side to side as he walked, as if the jerking motions of his head would prevent any thoughts, good or bad, from settling. He did a lap of the compound like this and then he ran into Towrag Charlie, who was picking invisible things out of his ear and putting them in his tobacco tin.

Towrag Charlie had a face which met in the middle. The description was Frank Morgan's and although the old man knew it didn't make sense, it fitted Towrag Charlie's face completely. Towrag's face never stopped moving. It folded itself up until the eyes, nose and mouth appeared to be all part of one line. 'Like a soup dish with a big handle at either end,' Frank had tried to explain. Towrag fell in beside the old man and they walked in silence.

Was the old man imagining things or was Towrag clean and tidy and wearing a collar and tie? He glanced sideways at his companion. Good God! Surely to heaven Towrag was not expecting a visitor. Who in the name of all that was holy would visit Towrag Charlie? But why else would he be here like this and wearing a collar and tie? It was no use asking him beause he would not understand. He had spent nearly forty of his sixty years in prison and somewhere along the way justice had exacted the last remnants of his mind.

The old man had heard Towrag's story a dozen times. He was a legend. They said there was not a screw from Brixton to Barlinnie who did not know him. Barker, the farm-screw, had said he was a fine-looking man when he was younger, full of fire.

He had deserted the army as a boy and they even said he had once killed a man. Not that anybody really knew, thought the old man. Not even Towrag himself could remember how it all began. It had taken five screws to put him out through the gate when his time was up just before Christmas. He had kicked and scratched like a wild man as they put him into the prison bus and drove him down to the railway station where they left him on a bench picking things from his ear. Two weeks later he was back inside with another five years to do for stealing a roll of grease-proof paper from Woolworth's.

But who could be visiting him? He had no relatives. And how could a man who had done forty-five years have any friends? The problem annoyed the old man. Always problems, always questions. What did it matter to him who was visiting Towrag Charlie? He was getting as bad as the rest of them.

They always had to know, didn't they? No matter how trivial it was, if it could be questioned they would ask to be told. The old man had watched them in the recreation hall, beckoning to each other, taking each other aside, a restless mass in search of information.

An extra table had been moved into the dining-hall with six extra chairs. Why? More men coming in, of course. But twenty-eight had gone out since the week-end and there would not be more than a dozen coming from the Scrubs tomorrow, there never was. So why the extra table? They called each other aside and asked each other what they had been talking about a moment before when they were called aside by somebody else and the questions and answers went round everybody, producing more questions which required more answers.

Towrag Charlie was all togged up for a visit.

'Holy cow, what sort of a mad bastard would visit Towrag for Christ's sake? Here! Here a minute, Taffy. No, Taffy, just a tick, over here. Towrag Charlie, Taffy. Who's his visit, Taffy? Aw for Christ's sake Taffy, you know me. Fuck you then. Bill! Over here a minute, Bill. Towrag Charlie, Bill. The soft bastard cow's got a visit . . . Taffy! Half a mo, Taffy. You want to watch that bastard, Taffy. What was he after over there? Snout? Then what, for Christ's sake? Bill! Keep your voice down, Bill. That Taffy bastard's been after you for snout, hasn't the cow? You lying bastard.'

What a way to be, thought the old man. Prying, poking, lying, abusing and all for something that didn't matter a tinker's damn. But who in the world could be visiting Towrag Charlie? Who in the world could find anything to say to a miserable brainless deadbeat like Towrag?

He left his silent companion and went to his room to collect his two library books. He still had half an hour before Jane and Tom arrived and if he didn't change them now he would have to wait until to-morrow night. He collected the books and climbed the

71

stairs to the tiny library on the first floor. Perhaps that new Alan Moorehead would be back in. His name was next on the list. He paused outside the library door for a moment to catch his breath. Then he went in.

The librarian smiled quickly in his direction and went back to explaining to the man standing at his desk that it was not the librarian's job to point out which books were dirtier than others. The librarian knew because he had read all of them but he had no intention of telling this fat, ignorant slob who probably couldn't read anyway. The fat man told the librarian that he had better watch his step if he didn't want this well-thumbed edition of *The Ginger Man* shoved up his arse and walked out with a pile of half a dozen books from the librarian's desk.

'Come back at once!' shouted the librarian, half rising from his stool. His piping voice sounded even fussier when he shouted. 'Come back at once! You know you are only permitted to take two books!' But the fat man was gone.

The librarian, just starting his last year of a six-year sentence for blackmail, had been a costing-clerk before he became a captive librarian and he had a clerical regard for order. He began his day with his desk and his mind in apple-pie condition and ended it with his whole library in confusion and his poor mind at breaking point.

The librarian, John, was everybody's dart-board. He was fussy and kind and helpful. He was tidy, the soft twerp, and he kept to the rules, minded his own business and kept a picture of his wife, who was ugly, on his desk. These things were all forgivable, of course. Not so John's enthusiasm for his job, his genuine regard for the books in his charge.

There was only one way to deal with that sort of thing: bugger up the works. Dust-jackets were there to be moved from Fiction to non-Fiction to Educational to Autobiographical. Moving these daft Georgette Heyers into Mechanical and Electrical would give the soft cow something to think about instead of sitting on his arse scribbling on little cards.

How about taking every other page out of this Edgar Wallace, who was a copper-loving bastard anyway, and gumming in every other page from this Ruby M. Ayres? Christ, what a joke! Here, just a minute! Then we'll get that crazy old bastard what's-'is-name from the boiler house to take it out. Bet you a roll-up the soft cow reads it and doesn't know the difference.

It was even more enjoyable to make fun of the librarian's enthusiasm. Seekers-after-knowledge-with-poker-faces were determined to make a go of it when they got out this time and felt that a familiarity with the theories of centre-lathe turning, nuclear physics or bird-watching would be helpful to them in beginning a new career. Could the librarian assist them in selecting the best works on these subjects? The librarian could, of course. He would spend hours of his own time selecting books, going through them to make sure they were not too advanced. He never learned, the librarian.

He was what they called a thick bastard because he believed what he was told. He even believed the seekers-after-knowledge-with-poker-faces when they came back and told him they had changed their minds about centre-lathe turning, nuclear physics and bird-watching and had decided to take up athletics.

The librarian ended his day dog-tired and confused and began the next replacing dust-jackets, moving books back to their proper places and ungumming alien pages. Life was a real struggle for the librarian. He did not understand.

The old man found the new Alan Moorehead and hunted along the rows for a second book. There were several other men in the library. Most of them worked in the cookhouse and were off duty until teatime. And most of them were gathered at the light-fiction shelves. Sex corner, they called it.

There was a desperation about the whole perform-ance because the library would soon be closing for the day. They riffled through book after book, their eyes darting into the pages for a phrase or a word which might indicate that they had found what they were looking for. 'Bed', for instance. Or 'breast', or 'switch off the lights', or 'she', or 'come here'. Or even 'they'. There it was: 'he slipped his hand . . . what about a second one?' What's this? 'Unexpurgated edition'? What the hell is that supposed to mean?

There were others who chose their reading by touch. By volume, really; size and weight. The old man selected a second book and walked to the librarian's desk. The man in front of him was taking out a huge volume on Egyptian architecture.

'Got it at last, eh,' said the librarian as the old man handed over his books to be marked. 'I think you'll like it.'

The old man said cheerio and left the librarian to the man behind, who wanted permission to take all umpteen volumes of *The World Atlas* back to his room so that he could put Wales in South America.

The old man put his books on his bed and reported to the duty-screw's office that he was expecting a visit.

'Markham, eh,' said the screw, looking down his list. 'Right, Markham. Wait outside with the others.'

A dozen or so men, their uniforms pressed and their hair, where they had any, slicked down with water, were assembled inside the main entrance hall. Except for the clacking of their heels as they walked up and down or round in small circles, there was no sound, no talking. One of the men carried a small pink carnation carefully in front of him, its stem wrapped in silver paper from a cigarette packet. Another man carried a wooden reading-lamp he had made in the prison hobbies class and which he had been allowed to buy out of his private funds for seven and sixpence, the price of the wood.

In turn the men moved casually past the glass doors from where they could see the main gates and the visitors who were beginning to arrive. They glanced quickly out of the sides of their eyes but didn't pause unless, every now and again, they recognised a visitor as their own. Frank Morgan came down the stairs and leaned on a wall, well away from the others. The old man pretended not to notice him. Frank was looking down at his shoes.

You could see the difference when a man knew his visitors had arrived. The tension left his face. He didn't exactly smile or say anything but his movements became fractionally jauntier. It was like a man being told his wife had had her first baby, thought the old man. He knew all along that everything would be all right but now he was a hundred per cent certain. The old man took his turn past the glass doors. A woman with a pink coat and a tall man. No, Tom was short and Jane wouldn't wear a pink coat. He hoped they had not been delayed in the traffic.

Towrag Charlie came into the entrance hall from the dining-room and went across to the duty-screw's office.

'Yes, Towrag,' said the screw. 'What can we do for you this fine sunny afternoon?'

'Visit, sir,' mumbled Towrag. The men in the entrance hall stopped moving.

'What!' It was almost a shout.

'Visit, sir,' repeated Towrag Charlie. The old man

heard the rustling of paper as the duty-screw flicked through the pages of his visits register.

'Christ almighty, Towrag. Here you are as big as life. Partridge. Well I'll be. . . .' So that was Towrag's name: Partridge.

The men in the entrance hall looked at each other, smiling. For once, the old man thought, nobody was questioning.

'All right, Mr Partridge,' said the duty-screw. 'If you will wait outside, I will call you.' He chuckled as Towrag left his office to join the other waiters, who had all resumed their walking.

The telephone in the duty-screw's office rang and everybody stopped walking again. After a few moments the screw put the phone down with a clank. 'Partridge! Smith! Jones! Porteous! Off you go!'

The four men hurried out into the sunshine and the rest resumed their walking. The old man took another turn past the doors. Towrag and the other three were just being let through the main gate and a woman with two small children had just got out of a car at the gatehouse. Still no sign of Jane and Tom. Dammit, you'd think they would arrive a little early just to be sure. Another minute and they would be late.

The telephone rang again and everybody was still. Then the screw put it down with another clank. 'Brooks! McNally! Away you go.'

Frank was still leaning against the wall looking at his shoes. He has not even bothered to tell the screw he is here, thought the old man. He must know they were not coming. Why did he punish himself and everybody else like this. The telephone went again.

'Campbell! Burns! Williams! Look sharp or there'll be no tea left.'

There were only four of them left now and the two other men were standing by the glass doors watching the gatehouse so that the old man would have had to ask them to move to see himself. They were two minutes late, damn them. All the best tables at the back would be gone and they would have to sit right under the visit-screw's nose. The old man could feel a lump, half of anger and half of fear, rising in his throat. One day a month and they couldn't even. . . . The telephone rang again and the old man waited with his heart thumping. 'Erikson! Bartholomew! Get going.' The screw slammed the receiver back into its cradle. 'Markham!'

The old man jumped at his own name. They were here. He walked past Frank Morgan without seeing him and out into the sunshine. A screw was holding the big, diamond-mesh gate open and Erikson and Bartholomew had just gone through. 'Hurry up, you!' the screw shouted to the old man, who broke into a shuffling run. He fished in the breast pocket of his jacket for his visit pass as he ran and waved it towards the screw as he passed.

'Just a minute, you,' said the screw. The old man stopped, agitated. The screw slammed the big gate shut and locked it with one of the keys hanging from his waist on a heavy chain. He did it slowly, pulling at the gate to make sure it was secure before slipping his keys into his trousers pocket. 'Let's have a look at that pass, you.'

The old man handed over the small square of paper. 'It's all right, sir. I applied to Mr Jenkins two weeks ago for a visit. My visitors have arrived.'

The screw continued to examine the square of paper on which was a name a date and the signature of Mr Jenkins. 'I'll decide what is all right, you.' The old man glanced anxiously towards the visiting-hut. Erikson and Bartholomew had already handed in their passes to the main guardroom and were going into the visiting-hut. This one was a pig all right. He had a nature like his face, which was as ugly as sin. 'All right, you,' said the screw, handing back the pass.

The old man took the pass and set off again at a run. 'Just a minute, you.' The old man stopped again, anger seething in him like a cauldron. If he had something in his hands he would smash it into this pig's sneering face. Visits were nothing to do with the bastard anyway.

'Walk,' said the screw. 'Don't run, walk.'

The old man walked off quickly and handed in his pass at the guardroom.

He walked round the other side of the building to the visiting-hut. He had been right. All the best tables were gone. The room was full of men, most of them from the other compounds. They sat at a table each, facing the small green door behind the visit-screw's desk through which their visitors would come. The old man found himself a table towards the front of the room and sat down to watch the door. His anger was going. In a moment Jane and Tom would be with him and for a while the world would not be grey.

CHAPTER 5

The women came in all ages, sizes, and conditions: shabby, flash, well groomed; haughty, at ease, nervous; pathetically poor to ostentatiously rich. They came with bewildered children and children who had seen it all before: babies in carrycots; teenage sons and daughters with hard faces, ashamed faces, tearful faces. They came in Jaguars with friends with sharp suits and shiny, matted black hair. They came in medium-sized family saloons with older friends in tweedy suits and with bald heads in Minis with their sisters, and in buses alone with yards of children.

This was the moment of truth, when 'You should see my bird' had to stand the test of dozens of pairs of prying, hungry eyes, and when a man had to steel himself against the unvoiced sniggers as his fat, frowzy wife dragged their six unkempt children across the room towards him. Make no mistake, thought the old man, everybody was looking and remembering.

There was pride, too, an indecent, sick pride in many cases, in the way young men preened themselves as their young, dyed-blonde women approached. And the women knew what the men were thinking, all the men. And many of them liked it. There was a lot of love, of course. There had to be for a woman to come a hundred miles by bus to see a man who had left her with nothing. There was greed as well because where there are rogues there is money or, at least, rogues' friends who sell second-hand cars and are loyal in their way to the fallen and the friends of the fallen. There was certainly hate, and ill-concealed hate very often. You could see it in the eyes of a daughter who had come because her mother wished it. There was pity, of a sort. And a lot of self-pity. There was laughter and tears and passion which stopped just short of outright indecency and which left behind it irritability and jealousy. There was even happiness for a few. The last visit before release, sweetheart. We'll never be away from each other again.

The women, the friends, and the children poured in from the waiting-room beyond the green door, and their husbands and friends and fathers greeted them according to their inclinations or their pride or their shame; with a kiss, with a peck on the cheek, a handshake, a squeeze of the arm, or a hello, or a nod of the head. A young man of about twenty-five with a shock of sandy hair sat down opposite Towrag Charlie and smiled. Towrag smiled back with his toothless face. McNally greeted his huge wife with a yell of delight and threw his eight children up and down two at a time until the visit-screw told him to sit down and behave himself. A well-dressed woman sat at the table next to the old man's. She asked her husband how he was and her husband said he was fine. Neither of them smiled.

The old man saw Tom first, all 'Harris' tweed jacket and moustache, his arms waving above his head with hands clasped like a boxer accepting the applause of his fans. He'd heard something! The old man felt the blood draining from his face. He's heard something already! He hardly saw Jane come into the room behind Tom and go with him to the visit-screw's desk to check in. Tom could have heard this morning from the Home Secretary. If only it were true. God, if only it were true. He wanted to run to them, to take Tom by the arm and shake him until he told him the Home Secretary had ordered his immediate release. But they would be here in a moment. For God's sake hurry up, the pair of you. Get a bloody move on you stupid bitch.

Jane walked towards him smiling, her head on one side. The old man tried to smile back but he could feel the muscles in his face twitching uncontrollably. She took him by the arms and stood on tiptoe to kiss him.

'Jimmy, darling, you look well.' He didn't want to ask. Why in hell's name couldn't she tell him. Tom had him by the hand, pumping it up and down and asking him how he was and slapping him on the shoulder with his other hand. The old man didn't want to ask. He wanted them to tell him and they wouldn't. They kept pawing at him and asking him how he was and telling him he looked well. They pulled him down into his chair and sat on the opposite side of the table, each holding one of his hands.

God but he looked well, didn't he. Tom had never seen him looking so well and Jane didn't think she had either. The old man felt like screaming at them. Why in hell's name did Jane bring this clown with her every time? He was always the same, always shouting, always back-slapping.

Tom stopped smiling, suddenly. 'No news yet, old man, I'm afraid.' Then he smiled again. 'But no news is good news!'

Jane tilted her head even more to one side. 'Darling, it's too early yet for us to have heard anything. We have everybody working for you. It won't be long now, Jimmy. Honest, darling, it won't be long.'

The old man felt his body relax. They were right, of course. It was too early for them to have heard and he had known so all along. But why all the victory-salute stuff of Tom's? Aw, what did it matter; there was no bad news anyway. They were obviously taking an interest in the case at the Home Office or they would have refused straight away. He felt better again and smiled at his wife and friend.

'That's better,' said Tom, squeezing the old man's hand. 'That's more like the Jimmy we know.'

The Jimmy they knew. Oh yes, that Jimmy. Some lifetimes ago there had been a Jimmy like that with good manners and a pleasant disposition. He had liked a man called Tom, a saloon-bar wag with an empty head and too much money he had never worked for. But a good-natured man who was always one of the first to offer help to the needy. Providing the needy had money as well, of course.

More spiritual help, really. People who needed taking out of themselves were Tom's meat. There had been a time after the old man's fall from grace, as Tom put it in the saloon of the 'Barley Mow', when Tom had not been around. The newspapers reported most of the after-court doings, that most of the debts had been paid with the sale of Jimmy's property and that the Stock Exchange had settled the rest. But there was no money left and Tom found difficulty in answering the telephone.

Then the newspapers had carried a paragraph saying that Jane had been left some thousands in a relative's will. She would not be rich but they would have plenty to live on when Jimmy came out. Tom found he was not so busy as he had thought. He even found time to put in a call to Jane. Then he found more time to organise the vicar into an angel of mercy who collected signatures and wrote heart-rending letters to the

Archbishop of Canterbury. Tom collected two signatures himself.

A good friend was Tom, who knew a man called Jimmy, who was not the same any more. And Tom could not understand, because to him men were black and white, and rich and poor, and wasn't that place pretty much like a holiday camp anyway. It was not quite a laughing joke, but it was a joke all the same.

Jane and Tom were giggling. They were looking past the old man's head and giggling like a couple of schoolchildren.

'What's the matter?' For a moment the old man had thought they were laughing at him but now he could see they were looking past him to one of the tables behind. He wanted to look round but he didn't dare. 'Tell me what's the matter,' he insisted, finding himself giggling as well. 'Come on, what's so funny?'

Tom took his handkerchief out of his pocket and blew his nose hard. He and Jane leaned over the table towards the old man and the old man leaned too until their heads were almost touching. 'Well,' whispered Tom in his saloon-bar story-teller's voice, 'it seems that the young man at the table right at the back of the room, in the corner you understand, is trying to remove his young lady's clothing. And she is seen to demur.'

They all giggled together. The old man looked at the visit-screw, who was looking towards the corner with a knowing smile on his face. Tom took a quick look over the old man's shoulder and crouched down again. The young man, he said, was insisting. In fact he had the young woman's bra undone and half-way out of the front of her blouse and she was frantically trying to tuck it out of sight and to keep his hand off the zip-fastener in her skirt with her other hand.

The old man heard a squeal of protest behind him and a curse. Then the visit-screw got up with a sigh from his desk and walked quickly to the corner. The old man turned round. He could see the girl, a brassy thing with pink curls, buttoning her blouse and obviously agitated. The screw, well aware by now that every eye in the room was on him, bent over the table.

'I think you had better leave, madam.' The young man was on his feet now, protesting loudly. The screw ignored him. 'I think you had better leave now, madam. You seem to have caused enough trouble.'

Now the girl, a big girl with square shoulders, was standing up and demanding to see the Governor because she was not going to be spoken to like that by a rotten screw as if she was one of the bloody rotten old lags.

Mrs McNally, who was with her brood at the very next table, rose slowly from her chair, spilling two children onto the floor. The sides of her mouth were drawn down and her enormous bosom was heaving with long-endured indignation. Who was a bloody rotten old lag; her Paddy? A right arm that had bathed, beaten, supported, and defended eight children almost alone and unaided for many years, caught the young woman on the side of the head and sent her crashing across the rickety table and into the arms of her young man, who was already verbally issuing several different kinds of writ, for defamation of character, bodily annoyance and damage to property — e.g. one wife. Paddy was offering to fight anybody, including the visit-screw, who was trying to wrest the young woman from the arms of her husband while keeping himself between the young woman and Mrs McNally, who was telling her husband to mind his own business. Shouts of 'Sit down you fat old bitch!' and, 'Give 'm hell Paddy!' and, 'For Christ's sake shut up!' came from all round the room.

The children, forgotten in the excitement, had moved up closer to the action, which promised to become even more interesting now the young woman had regained her feet. She seemed to be manœuvring for an opening in the fat one's guard. Or was she staggering?

The old man was enjoying himself. Not because he liked violence, he hated it, but because for the first time Jane and Tom could see what it was really like in here. He was not telling them about it and seeing the half-formed looks of disbelief on their faces, the oh-but-the-governor-is-a-sweetie, and the that-little-fat-officer-from-Yorkshire-seemed-a-very-pleasant-little-man looks. They were laughing now all right but when they got home they wouldn't laugh. Not after they had thought about it and come to realise how terrible it was to laugh at all.

Or would they? Would they laugh more when they got home and more still as they told others the story, duly embroidered? Would they tell the vicar with his solemn petition and would the vicar laugh? And would everybody laugh and say it was not so bad for old Jimmy? Quite a giggle, really. He wanted to tell Jane and Tom it was not funny but he couldn't stop laughing himself and anyway he didn't know how to begin.

He didn't want to say 'now look here you don't know the half of it: this is not a joke.' He wanted to say 'this is a joke all right but a hellish joke and don't run away with the idea that anybody here is laughing for fun'. But he couldn't because he couldn't stop laughing. His sides and throat were aching with laughing. As a matter of fact he was not enjoying himself. He didn't think Mrs McNally was funny.

James Hubert Markham, humanitarian, wanted to tell Jane and Tom that if they really wanted to hear something funny they should talk to Bert. No, he wanted to punch them in their faces and say 'laugh at that'. Why not? It hurt, didn't it? Even more than that he wanted to get up and walk away, to check out with the visit-screw and leave them giggling to each other.

But the visit-screw was busy. Mrs McNally was beating him over the head with a string bag of vegetables. Another screw had come through from the waiting-room and was trying to placate the young woman with promises that she could have another visit next week if only she would leave now, peacefully. The young woman told him he was a son-of-a-bitch and a licensed crook.

What a way to earn a living!

The old man knew most of the screws by sight and by name but he knew little about them. He knew they lived in semi-detached houses just up the road with their wives and children and dogs and cats and that some of them were bluff and some solemn and some neither. They were all shapes and sizes and ages and they all looked different in their civvies. Yet they were all the same.

Most of them were doing life with a number of weeks' remission every year and two days' free association with the human world every week unless they did overtime, as most of them did because there are not too many men like them.

Time affected them as much as it did the con. It made them easy-going and gentle, or suicidal. It made them surly and vicious and mad.

The new recruits had a shamefaced look about them, their moral fibre as uncreased as their uniforms. They were a little too friendly or a little too bossy, depending on their inclinations or their ambitions, but they would soon learn that neither is appreciated, that the life of an officer in H.M. Prison Service, from the Governor to the cookhouse number two, is fifty per cent solitary confinement, twenty-five per cent disgust, and the rest total indifference, with the odd kick in the face to remind one that all is subhuman under the regulation prison hat.

They carried their scars like war wounds: Lost that rib in Dartmoor, 1943; See that scar? Parkhurst on an outside working party. The bastard came at me with a shovel. No, thought the old man, there was no freedom here. For anybody. Even the prison chaplain with his soapy sermons was a prisoner of his God or his conscience or something. Even that big fat cat in the cookhouse was called Grievous Bodily Harm.

The Governor came in with the chief officer and together they herded the battlers between the tables and out into the waiting-room. The young man and his wife were sobbing at each other and even Mrs McNally's indignation was spent. The children followed in a confused line with their father behind telling them to pick their feet up and never to trust a bloody screw. It was never too early to put a child on the right path and they already knew about coppers being bastards. The chief officer smiled back into the visiting-room and closed the green door behind him.

The old man and his wife and friend had tea and ate their chicken sandwiches and buns with fresh cream. They didn't speak. They watched the others. Not directly, but with sweeping, disinterested glances.

The couple at the next table were talking quietly about financial arrangements and schools for sons, in spite of everything, and insurance policies. Fathers played awkward games with young children, women sobbed, and flash young men, too much at ease to be new to it all, laughed out loud and flicked crumbs away from the sleeves of their suits.

They had brought illustrated catalogues for Mercedes-

91

Benzs and Jaguars and other young men with nothing in their pockets but a rough, blue handkerchief and an empty tobacco tin, smoked Player's Perfectos and said that was the car for them and they had better put an order in as soon as they were due out in 1969. The earnestness in their faces and in the movements of their hands begged for agreement that four years to go was not a long time; only three Christmasses because they would be out on December twenty-third. What a Christmas Eve that would be. Four summers, three springs and only three winters. Only so many more visits, only so many more weekly letters. Only, only, only.

Young women on stiletto heels teetered to the tea counter waving their bottoms and came back to agree, smiling, that it was only. And to tell about the big opening-night at Jack Thing's — you remember Jack Thing! — new club, when champagne flowed like water. And how they all went to Brighton in Diana's boy's new drophead Chevvy and had a Chinese meal and too much to drink and had to stay the night. Which was miserable really because you were not there, honey. But wasn't it a scream when Di walked into the wrong bedroom, Harry? It was, agrees Harry, flicking more crumbs away from his jacket. But not much of a gas really because you were not there old fellow to do your imitations of Fred Emney and Max Bygraves.

And four years becomes four years. Forty-eight months, forty-eight more visits. Two hundred and eight more letters, three damned Christmasses and damned nearly, four, one thousand, four hundred and sixty more shaves. More and more and more. And who gives a bloody curse.

Mr Dandridge the welfare officer was the thinnest man in the world. He was also, the old man thought, one of the most unlovely. He was practically without hair, walked with a pronounced limp, smelled of garlic and spoke with a whining voice.

The welfare officer was making his way round the room from table to table, approaching each with his head on one side and a puzzled expression on his face in case of a bereavement. The old man watched him operate along the tables by the opposite wall, a quick word here and there, very often to the back of somebody's head, and a smile when he was sure that nobody was dead.

Frank Morgan had a theory about the welfare officer which was based on the assumption that after taking one step forward and two back for twenty years he had been reduced insensible to either abuse or reason. Frank had said that if Dr Gallup took a poll in here to measure the relative popularity of Mr Dandridge and the tread-mill, the treadmill would come out on top. Mr Dandridge was full of good intentions which had come through twenty years of bombardment with every kind of spleen and invective almost untouched. But he had no more idea how to find the right job for the right old lag than the old lag had intentions of working. Put Mr Dandridge anywhere and he would be in the way. Give

Mr Dandridge a problem to iron out and you could bet your boots by the end of the week you would have lost your wife, your children, your remission and, in all probability, your reason. Frank had strong opinions on the welfare officer. But the old man was sure it could not always have been so with Mr Dandridge.

He must have begun with the stock mission and the stock desire to bring some small comfort. Mr Dandridge could not have known in those days that he was embracing a profession which dealt almost exclusively in failure, a job which required one to persuade an adamant and dedicated thief from being a bank manager, or a sex maniac from running an orphanage. It would have been a challenge in those days, the meaty, manly task of making leather purses out of sows' ears. Except that they nearly all wanted to be silk purses or to be left as sows' ears.

So Mr Dandridge was digging a hole close to where a thousand lags were digging another hole. Mr Dandridge had nowhere to put his dirt and the lags had nowhere to put theirs except on top of Mr Dandridge's. The higher the welfare officer rose from the root of the problem, the lower the lags sunk.

The old man smiled at the thought and Jane, who was still holding his hand across the table, asked gently what he was smiling at. 'I'm in the snooker final tonight,' the old man said. 'I get an ounce of tobacco if I win and I can swap it for a pot of Marmite and some marmalade.'

Jane squeezed his hand and said that was nice and they would be keeping their fingers crossed for him. Tom chuckled and said, 'Don't eat it all at one sitting.' They had nothing left to say to each other. Jane and Tom had told the old man what they had had for lunch and they had described their drive down in detail. The old man had told them about the snooker, which was all he could remember of the mental list he had made.

He wanted them to leave because until they left they could not get news from the Home Secretary or the Archbishop. Suppose there had been a telephone call at home while Jane was out!

The visit-screw stood up and clapped his hands. 'Sorry, ladies and gentlemen. Time's up!'

Almost everybody in the room stood up immediately and moved closer together in groups. Young men and young women grasped each other and kissed violently, pressing their bodies hard together. Children watched and giggled and scrambled under and around the tables. Men grasped handfuls of cigarette butts from the ash-trays and stuffed them into their hip pockets, spreading them so as not to make an obvious bulge. They stuffed biscuits and cakes into their mouths while the women wept. The room was alive with movement. Men scratched their legs and dropped things inside their stockings; rolled pound notes into tiny balls and slipped them under their tongues; felt under the clothes of their women while the women slipped an ounce of tobacco inside their shirts. And the visit-screw didn't look because he knew and everybody knew that he knew. They would take their chance of being one of the six chosen to be given a dry bath in the search-room.

Some of the women had left already, including the unsmiling woman from the table next to the old man's. Towrag Charlie's visitor shook him by the hand and said something the old man could not hear, but Towrag smiled as the young man left. The visit-screw moved about the room saying, 'Break it up!' and 'That will be enough now', and 'You'd better run after your mum, sonny; she's gone'. The old man kissed his wife and shook hands with his friend, who was patting him on the back again.

As they left he moved over to the windows to watch them walk down by the fence to the car park. Jane kept stopping to wave and the old man wished she would go. She should have left somebody at home to answer the telephone.

He watched them drive off and his arm was aching with waving. Then the visit-screw ordered them all into a line and ran his hands over each of them as they moved outside.

'What's this?'

'A picture of my kids, sir.'

'Okay. What's this?'

'The new Mercedes-Benz, sir.'

'You've got delusions, haven't you? What's this?'

'Cigarette ends, sir.'

'Throw them back and whatever you've got in the

top of your sock. Cough! Ah, a pound note. Wonder how that got there? Report to the office for a dry bath, lad. You're in trouble. You, dry bath. You've got a lumpy chest, lad. Dry bath. And don't try to ditch the "Old Holborn" on the way, the Governor's outside.' The visit-screw smiled at the old man. 'Any opium or flick-knives, Markham? Okay, old son, away you go.'

James Hubert Markham, from near-poverty in Wandsworth, S.W., to Lombard Street, to a joke, in sixty-something years. He could still remember the cold, Dickensian day in God-knows-what year he walked into the office of Percy C. Tredegar, his first employer, in Lombard Street and met money face to face. He was fourteen, thin, plain, the son of a low-grade civil servant and a Welsh mother with ambitions. And blue with cold.

Percy C. Tredegar sat behind wide, velvet collars and a thick curtain of cigar smoke through which young James could see the flicker and glow of a fire which probably cost more by the day than he was about to earn by the week. Young James did not make the economic comparison on the spot but he realised it later as he in his turn told his success story to cold, skinny boys from behind a cloud of cigar smoke.

It was a story of James Hubert Markham, of Wandsworth, S.W., becoming James H. Markham & Co. of Lombard Street. Assets: glib tongue, strong stomach, brass neck and a well-oiled ear to the ground. Going from strength to strength, buying shares, issuing shares, more shares, more shares, more shares . . . and it was hardly true, was it.

His widowed Welsh mother had had the backbone and Jane had had the brass neck. For quite a time he had been in the middle, batted backwards and forwards between the two of them as if they were afraid that to let him be still for a moment would end his financial ascendancy. And they were right.

The mother died complaining and the wife kept batting; with Harrods, Regent Street furniture, hair appointments twice a week, week-ends in Paris, two cars changed regularly and, finally, the near-mansion in the stockbroker belt. The cost of living rose and the wife batted harder. But the ball was getting lumbago and rheumatism in one leg and its judgement was not as sound as it had been. Finally, its nap worn to a thin fuzz, it rolled to a stop. Thirty thousand pounds' worth of other people's property had been misappropriated. The cars went first, then the furniture, then the mansion and then the old man himself.

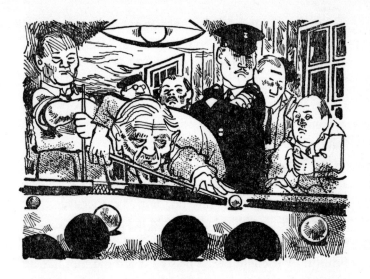

CHAPTER 6

Jenkins, little, fat and dapper, sat on the end of the billards table picking his nose. He was listening to a young man, Weatherslade, who was asking him not to sit on the table at it had just been brushed in readiness for the snooker final. The young man smiled an enthusiastic smile at Jenkins, who said 'Piss off'. Then Jenkins smiled a sneering, dirty smile. His finger was still in his nose.

The old man hated Jenkins more than anything else in the world. He loathed and detested Jenkins and wished him in terrible pain. The sight of the back of his flat head was enough to send the old man into an inner fury which left him bereft of thoughts of what he would like to happen to the man.

He had never seen Jenkins perform one half-decent act or heard him utter a word which was not like a slap in the face to somebody. Jenkins, the old man knew, was evil. He was the only one hundred per cent bad man he had ever met and there was no room in his mind for doubt.

Just look at him now. The old man wanted Weatherslade to hit Jenkins, to jab out his evil eyes with one of the billiards cues. But no, not Weatherslade. Not enthusiastic Weatherslade, an old lag at twenty-six and enjoying it for everybody to see. He was so bloody brimful of friendliness he blasted it around him like an aerosol through a mouthful of broken teeth. Nobody would tell Weatherslade to piss off, except Jenkins.

Weatherslade had never been heard to talk of getting out or even to indicate that he knew there was any such place as outside. He called everybody over thirty, 'sir', and most people, including Jenkins, knew he was not taking the piss. He was a trusty with a red band on his arm and this red band was to him what the Field-Marshal's baton is to the Sandhurst cadet, only more so.

He played football for his hut and any other hut that would have him. He played cricket for the prison eleven against visiting teams and treated the affairs as if he were personally welcoming the Harrow eleven to the playing-fields of Eton. He played chess expertly and let the old men win, and he was captain of the darts team

from number three compound. Weatherslade intro-
duced volley ball to number two compound, won the
billiards championship at Easter, cleaned the Church of
England chapel twice a week, and unaided, laid a bowl-
ing green for the old lags of number four compound.
He was leader of the music appreciation circle, the quiz
team and the reading circle. And he had organised the
snooker competition.

The old man could see Weatherslade was confused,
struggling in his mind to remember how he could have
offended. He was twice the size of Jenkins and his
broken nose and teeth indicated that he had come up
the hard way. Yet he was gentle in a boisterous sort of
way. 'We must get the table cleared, sir,' he said to
Jenkins. 'The match starts in fifteen minutes, you know.'

Jenkins made no move to get down. He put his fore-
finger against Weatherslade's chest and pushed. 'Piss
off.' The younger man moved back a step, still puzzled
and still smiling. He looked towards where the old man
was sitting by the radio and then back at Jenkins.

'Please sir, we must . . .'

'Piss off.' The smile had disappeared from Jenkins's
face. His eyes were narrowed and his bottom jaw was
jerking nervously.

Something slipped in or out of place in the old man
and he jumped to his feet and half ran across the room.
He pushed Weatherslade aside and looked fiercely at
the little man perched on the edge of the table.

'Get off there, you damned swine!'

He knew it sounded ridiculous and pompous but it was the worst thing he could think of. Obscenities had no meaning here. They were part of normal conversation, used on friends as friendly greetings and farewells, almost as endearments. But swine was a detestable word, the most insulting the old man had ever heard and he had never used it on anybody before in his life.

Jenkins was laughing his sneering laugh, the swine, the swine. The miserable little swine.

'Piss off.'

The old man could feel hysteria rising in himself. Jenkins' forefinger was on his chest, pressing him away. There was a redness in front of his eyes and his hands clawed at each other. Every indignity and grudge and pain was centred in the sneering face in front of him. The face embodied everything that he had endured or imagined, ever. Jenkins represented not only a threat to his liberty to play snooker, but a threat to his sanity. He wanted to get his hands up to the man's face, to claw out his evil eyes. But somebody was pulling him away. Somebody had hold of him from behind and was pulling him slowly back to his seat by the radio. He was sitting down and his hands and knees were trembling like mad things.

'Sit still, Jimmy. Sit still for a minute.' It was Bert's voice. Bert's big hands pushed him back into the chair and he could see more men were gathered round muttering sympathy and saying a chap of his age shouldn't be here, those crooked, bastard coppers. He closed his eyes and opened them again and he could see more clearly. He saw Bert walk over to the billiards table and he saw Bert's huge fist smack into Jenkins' face, sending him spinning off the edge of the table and into a corner. He saw Bert lean over the cringing figure and say something, and a feeling of immense satisfaction came over him.

Yes, Bert, he would be all right for the game. He smiled at the men, who were patting him on the back and telling him he was a foxy old bastard.

Jenkins was sitting in a darkened corner dabbing at his nose with his rough, blue handkerchief.

There they were, those two pompous nits who had shared his walk before breakfast. They had found two more for bridge. Know-all Knowles, stuffed with useless facts from his scrawny neck to the top of his bald head, was holding court by the dart-board. The old man chuckled to himself. Old Know-all always managed to gather the dimmest buggers in the prison around him when he held court. Those two with him now weren't impressed by Know-all's knowledge, for God's sake. They couldn't understand a thing he was talking about. It seemed such a waste.

Weatherslade was going over the billiards table again with a brush, whistling a hundred miles out of key. He scrubbed at the faded green baize so hard, the screw on duty at the door came across and told him not to rub the bloody thing down to the slate. 'Yes, sir. Right you are, sir.' The screw walked back to his seat just outside the door and Weatherslade brushed on with exaggerated gentleness which in anybody else would have been taken for dumb insolence. But Weatherslade didn't have an insolent bone in his body and the screw knew it.

The old man looked up at the clock by the door. Five minutes to go before the match was due to start. Some of the men were already gathering round the table to make sure of a ringside seat. Taffy was there, of course. It was funny about Taffy. His eyes were never still, which was odd for a man whose sole purpose in life seemed to be to observe and describe inanimate objects, which everybody could see for themselves anyway.

His eyeballs seemed to roll round and round as if they were trying to manœuvre the object of his interest into the right position for observing. It was all so mindless. Unless the man had a fear of blindness or something and had to keep proving to himself that he could distinguish the smallest detail. Yes, that could be it. Now he thought about it, the old man thought he might have noticed from time to time a certain weakness about Taffy's eyes. They were very pale eyes.

Down at the other end of the big room about a hundred men were watching one of those quiz shows on television, one of those shows where the questions were easy and all you had to do to win was to make a national fool of yourself and swap humour with the compère, who was already established. It was one of the most popular shows of the week. Probably, the old man thought, because it dealt with luxury. The men were laughing and slapping their thighs and explaining to each other what had happened. He was a card all right, this one. He could give as good as he took and no mistake. It reminded the old man of that joke he had heard told in his club where this man was boasting about his brother's repartee and command of the English language. And quick as a flash my brother said 'piss off'.

Jenkins, still dabbing at his blackened nose with his handkerchief, minced across and sat on the chair next to the old man, who didn't look at him. For some moments Jenkins didn't say anything then: 'You don't want to have anything to do with these bastards, Markham. They're pigs, dirty old towrags, the lot of 'em.' The old man didn't want to listen. He was enjoying himself just looking forward to the game. He looked around for Bert and spotted him over by the snooker table talking with Weatherslade and he wished Bert would turn round and see that Jenkins was bothering him again.

'Rotten pigs, the lot of 'em. Dirty old towrags.' Jenkins pressed his handkerchief under his nose and put his head back for a moment. 'I don't give a fuck for 'em. I'm not sorry for anything, I've had my good times. The best motors, the best women.' He blew his nose and winced with the pain. 'The best food, the best booze. Dirty towrags, the lot of 'em. Wouldn't give 'em the pickin's out of me nose. Swine. Eh? Eh?'

The old man made a non-committal noise with his throat and stood up to go over to Bert and Weatherslade. Jenkins got up with him. 'Just a minute, Markham. Game doesn't begin yet. You goin' to win?' He gave a sneering laugh and Markham looked down at him.

'I shall do my best,' he said. Jenkins laughed again, more loudly this time.

'Not with an ounce of snout on it you ain't. Beardmore likes his burn. Them others knew they couldn't win in the end.'

The old man walked away leaving Jenkins still laughing his sneering laugh. What did he mean? Was the little swine saying the others had lost on purpose? Was that it? Ridiculous!

Bert moved around the table urging the men farther back to make room for the players. 'Farther back lads, come on. Give them room. Shove 'em back, Taffy.'

The thin man who always acted as marker had taken the rest from under the table and stationed himself by the marker board with the rest at a sentry's at-ease position. Bert shouted for silence and announced that the Governor and his lady would be across later to present the prizes and because it was already eight-thirty the chief had given permission for cocoa to be served at nine-fifteen instead of nine o'clock. Everybody clapped and cheered and said wasn't the chief the last word in poxy generosity.

The old man was hunting through the pile of cues by the marker board, trying to find the one he always used which was straight. Damn it, it wasn't there. His fingers were fumbling and nervous and he felt embarrassed as he picked one cue after another and sighted along it with his eye. Oh Christ, Beardmore had it. He must have put it aside earlier or asked someone to look after it for him. The old man took another cue. This one would have to do even if it was bent like a banana.

The chief gave the old man half a crown to toss with and the coin felt strange and heavy in his hand. He lost the toss.

'You go,' said Beardmore and turned and sat down.

The old man put the white ball in the half-circle and manœuvred it into position with his cue. He bent his knees and sighted along the cue, seeing the bow in it clearly now. Christ, what a cue. His legs were quivering and he heard someone giggle behind him. Jenkins, probably. The swine. He stabbed stiffly at the ball, feeling the cue jar in his right hand as it made contact out of true. But it was straight enough. The white ball struck the red triangle cleanly on the right-hand side, flicked away to the back cushion and came back off the side cushion down the table, still moving quite fast. Safe enough. No! The white struck the brown in front of his nose and rolled slowly into the bottom pocket to his left.

'Four away,' said the thin man and turned to adjust the board.

The old man sat down and somebody patted him on the shoulder. 'Bad luck, James. Damned bad luck, sir.'

Beardmore walked round the table pushing his straight cue backwards and forwards between the thumb and forefinger of his left hand. He stopped by the reds and leaned backwards with his cue extended over the table and towards a red which had been pushed well clear. He sucked his bottom lip and dropped quickly on to his haunches. After a few moments he straightened easily and walked back to the bottom of the table.

He flicked the white out of the pocket, catching it under the tip of his cue with which he rolled it deftly into position. He leaned over the table with his head held high, squinting down his nose at the ball. He hit it hard and cleanly. The white sped up the table and flicked the lone red into the back of the pocket with a crack. The white itself came off the cushion and back in an arc into the assembled reds, spreading them precisely.

Beardmore walked up the table and lined up on the black, a sitter. He hit it hard with back spin leaving the white three inches back from the point where it made contact with the black. Taffy took the black out of the pocket and already Beardmore had lined up on another red, perfectly positioned by the top left-hand pocket. The red went down cleanly and Beardmore crossed over once again and potted the black into the opposite pocket. Without hesitating he crossed over once again to the white, perfectly positioned once more for another red.

Beardmore pushed his spread, left hand across the worn baize, making a neat bridge between the nail of his arched thumb and the second knuckle of his fore-finger. He dropped the cue neatly into the bridge and ran it easily backwards and forwards, stopping the tip a fraction of an inch short of the ball each time. The expression on his sallow face was unchanged. It was not an expression at all, really.

Beardmore stepped away from the table and looked across it to the marker board. He narrowed his eyes as if trying to calculate and the old man looked at the board too. There was nothing to calculate, for God's sake. Markham nil, Beardmore a free four plus a break that looked like being a hundred. The old man was getting exasperated at the shuffling and whispering behind him, the gasps of admiration for a shot you could have blown in, for Christ's sake. And where the hell was Beardmore's problem? The damned red was sitting on the edge and the black was waiting again to follow with more reds and more blacks until the cows came home. Beardmore was looking round the table at the other balls. Holy Christ! What was he trying to do, get the whole bloody lot in with one shot? The whole bloody thing was a farce; the game itself was for layabouts, after all. Christ, he should have told them what to do with their championship. He could have been in bed reading his new book. Put the red in the pocket you self-satisfied nit.

Beardmore lined up again on the red, the fingers of

his left hand, stubby, athletic fingers, drumming on the baize. Again he hit the ball hard. The red caught the neck of the pocket, thudded from side to side in the narrow opening and came to rest hanging over the edge. The audience applauded and gasped and said 'Well, for Christ's sake!' and 'I'll be damned'. One or two laughed. Not hearty laughs, or hard-luck-mate laughs, but knowing laughs that set the old man's nerves jangling. Beardmore shook his head slowly without altering his non-expression, then turned quickly and sat down with a flourish.

'Sixteen,' called the thin man. He turned to adjust the board. 'Beardmore twenty, Markham nil.'

The old man walked quickly to the top of the table, his knees trembling. He stretched over the table towards the white and stabbed at it without bothering to take aim. The red dropped into the pocket and the white came off the top-cushion too fast to be in line for the black.

'One,' said the thin man.

Was that a laugh? The old man's fingers were trembling now. He looked hard at the white ball and then at the thin man, who called out for silence. That was a giggle! That was Jenkins all right. The fat, ignorant, loud-mouthed swine. All right Jenkins, you bastard. The old man called for pink. It was a difficult shot into the centre pocket and he would have to cut it fine. The pink went in neatly and the audience applauded, loudly. Too loud, was it? To hell with it.

'Seven,' called the marker.

The old man took an easy red and then the black. He took another red and then the black again, another red and then the pink, awkwardly. It teetered on the edge and rolled in.

Somewhere, somebody said, 'Lucky bastard', and somebody else said 'Shut your face you cow, or I'll shut it for you'.

'Thirty,' called the thin man.

Beardmore, his slippered feet stretched out in front of him and his cue resting across his paunch, clapped his hands and said 'Nice shot, Jimmy'. The white followed the next red into the pocket.

'Minus four makes twenty-six,' called the marker. 'Beardmore twenty, Markham twenty-six.'

The old man sat down and stretched his legs out in front of him, resting his cue across his narrow stomach. What about that, eh? Twenty-six and damned unlucky not to be more. Look at the marker board, Jenkins, you fat oaf. He could see Jenkins out of the corner of his eye, grinning. Always grinning and edging his fat stomach into you and complaining and arguing. Nobody was good or nice or kind according to you, Jenkins, with your fat prancing legs and the dirty little newspaper-clipping in your back pocket which described how a copper who once arrested you died in a cinema fire. You're a wrong worthless pig, Jenkins.

Beardmore made a break of twenty-eight, leaving only the colours on the table. He propped his cue in a corner and leaned on the wall close to the scorer and rolled a thick cigarette. Beardmore always rolled thick cigarettes and he always threw away the butts. Tow-rag Charlie and Sam followed in his wake like vultures. They shared the spoils without argument. The old man had heard it said that they could make three roll-ups each out of one of Beardmore's butts.

'Beardmore forty-eight, Markham twenty-six.' Don't you know anything, you skinny twerp? You should call the score of the one who spots off, first. Bloody idiot.

The old man was in a good position for the yellow but he walked up the table to check that he would not be snookered for the green afterwards. There was that sniggering again. Christ, they made nonsense of every-thing. They didn't laugh when Beardmore examined his position, did they? Why not? Why bloody not, eh? Because he was something else again, wasn't he?

The yellow went down and the audience applauded. 'Good old Jimmy.'

'Well done, James, you cunning old bastard.' 'Polish 'em off old fella.'

He poked the green into the same pocket and watched the white come back and push the brown hard against the side-cushion.

'Double it Jimmy,' someone said through the applause.

'Five,' called the thin man, banging his rest on the

wooden floor for silence. 'Quiet please, gentlemen. Beardmore forty-six, Markham thirty-three.'

The old man hammered the white towards the brown as hard as he could. It hit the brown at the right angle and it rebounded into the centre pocket opposite. Two screws had pushed their way through to be close to the table and they were clapping with the rest.

'Bloody beautiful shot you cunning old devil.'

'Jammy son of a bitch you clever old, old man you. Old man, you old man you. You can't keep a good old man down old man old man. . . .'

'Beardmore forty-eight, Markham thirty-six.'

The blue, where in hell's name is the blue? Christ, look at that blue. I could blow it in from here. He potted the blue and followed the white as it rolled up the table. His legs were shaking and so were his hands.

'Beardmore forty-eight, Markham thirty-nine.'

The old man looked at the marker board and at Beardmore and the thin man. Beardmore was still leaning on the wall puffing at his thick, misshapen cigarette. Beardmore usually made them neater than that surely? Certainly he did. The pink was lying awkwardly against the cushion but it was in line with the white for the top right-hand pocket. It was a good shot, just the right speed. The pink rolled along the cushion and dropped into the pocket. The applause hurt the old man's ears but he could hear no voices behind it, no laughs, no giggles.

The thin man pounded on the floor with his rest again and shouted: 'Beardmore forty-eight, Markham forty-five. The game is on the black ball.'

The rest, he would need the rest, somebody said. Give the old man the rest. Then there was complete silence. The old man could not see Jenkins. The thin man slid the rest across the table towards him.

The black was close to the side-cushion and about a foot from the top left-hand pocket. The white was almost two feet past the centre spot. He pushed the rest towards the white and dropped the cue into the fork. It jumped out again and juddered on the baize sending up tiny puffs of chalk. The old man froze, waiting. Nothing. He pushed the cue into the brass fork with both hands and took aim down it at the black, allowing the bow in the cue to drop to its own level. He could feel his legs quivering violently as he stretched on tip-toe over the table and stroked gently at the white. Too slow. Christ Almighty, too bloody slow. The white nudged the black towards the hole. A perfect shot, but too swining slow. The black stopped on the lip of the pocket.

Nobody gasped; nobody applauded. Beardmore looked at the old man but his look said nothing, as usual. He pushed himself off the wall and looked at the marker board and then at the black ball. Then he picked up his cue and potted it gently.

Beardmore and the old man shook hands and went

to where the Governor and his wife were sitting. Everybody applauded, including Jenkins, who was laughing. The Governor handed Beardmore two half-ounce packets of 'Old Holborn' and Beardmore said 'Thank you, sir', and half-bowed towards the Governor's wife. The chief stood behind, smiling. 'Bad luck, Markham,' said the Governor. 'A very close game indeed.' He gave the old man a voucher for a shilling to spend at the canteen and everybody cheered again and said 'Good old Jimmy!' because the Governor's lady was present.

James Hubert Markham filled his mug with cocoa from the big urn and sat down while the screws came round and counted him. They lost count and began again, taking a section of the tables each and counted with their fingers stabbing at each number and their lips moving. Then they all went into a huddle at the centre of the room, lifting their hats and scratching their heads and broke up taking a different section each. They finished counting again and met in the middle again and one of them walked off quickly towards the duty-screw's office.

'Somebody's away,' said Frank Morgan. 'Prepare yourself to be put to bed at the double.' The old man didn't smile because he didn't feel like smiling.

The screw came back with the chief and the counting began all over again. The chief was not smiling. 'Right. Everybody to your rooms and be quick about it.'

Everybody moved slowly, scraping their chairs across the floor and stacking them by the walls. The chief shouted for more speed so they moved a little more slowly, forgot their drinking mugs and went back for them, swept crumbs from the tables whether they were there or not and straightened the long strips of matting in the aisles between the tables.

Somebody was away. George? Could be, thought the old man. He hadn't seen him all evening. But he didn't really care. He felt as old as Egypt.

Everybody was laughing because somebody was away. He had taken advantage of the snooker finals and gone through the wire, which was clever, and he would be brought back, which was funny. The chief was as mad as a wet hen, wasn't he? He was mad because he had been smiling and clapping round the snooker table with the Governor and his wife while some cunning bastard was having it away. The soft cow. Holy Christ, just look at that sour-faced collection of bastard screws. Brains? Christ, they couldn't keep rabbits.

CHAPTER 7

Mrs Carpenter had been playing chess with a man who could neither read nor write and she had been well beaten in three straight games. The man had had a flat, unintelligent face and a coarse, unfriendly voice but Mrs Carpenter had liked him. He had told her that he was illiterate and that he had served twenty-five years altogether for an endless list of petty offences. The value of all the stolen goods involved in all the offences, the man had said, could not have come to more than five hundred pounds, which worked out at roughly twenty pounds a year. She had felt an almost overwhelming pity for him and she had been glad that he had won.

Mrs Carpenter was a prison visitor and once a month

she and a dozen friends from the villages came to the prison to play chess for two hours. It had been quieter tonight because of the snooker final in the dining-hall. Half the chess boards laid out in the visit-hut had been unused but that smug young man Bellingham whose father owned the local marine works had played three men at once on three separate boards, beating them all with ease. Bellingham was quite brilliant. Mrs Carpenter disliked him intensely for his cockiness and even more for the way he tried to make men who were already at the bottom feel lower.

She climbed into her little blue Mini outside the gate-house as Bellingham roared past in his sports car, sending a shower of gravel over the men going back through the big gates. She wondered why he came. Not, she was sure, for love of humanity. He seemed to go out of his way to show off his worldly advantages to a captive audience with nothing. Her husband said the boy had a brilliant future and Mrs Carpenter did not doubt it.

A prison officer came out from the gatehouse with a torch and shone it into the back seat of her car. 'We've lost one, Mrs Carpenter,' he said, chuckling. 'Just making sure he's not hiding in your car.' He said good night and moved with his torch to the car behind and Mrs Carpenter pulled out into the narrow country lane, waving good night to the elderly woman in the car behind.

Mrs Carpenter thought of her son away at Oxford and her husband up in Manchester on a business trip. Honest men. Except that her husband had stolen apples when he was a boy and Tim, just before he went up to Oxford, had taken a car which did not belong to him. She could still remember the numbing fear that had taken hold of her that day when it looked for a moment as if John would not be able to smooth things over with the owner, would not be able to keep his son out of court. They had held tightly to one another, the three of them, feeling the world underneath them crumbling. By unspoken agreement they never mentioned the subject again. What had that man stolen, the one who was illiterate? Eggs, he had said. Two years in a borstal institution for half a dozen eggs then three more years for half a hundredweight of lead. And nobody to hold on to to stop the world from crumbling.

The night was clear and Mrs Carpenter drove slowly, keeping the headlights of her car dipped. There was still an ache of pity in her throat for the crude man who could not read or write. And now there was another escape. Somewhere out here in the darkness some poor soul was hiding. A thief? Probably. A man who had been greedy for something which belonged to somebody else. Money, most likely. Or a car, perhaps. She wanted the man to be comfortable, to reach his wife and sons and daughters, and to escape to some happy place.

She swung the little car round the hairpin bend by the old church, flicking the headlights on to full beam with her foot. The old stone church pulled away from her in a blur of foggy light and as she levelled out she dipped the headlights. She only caught a fleeting glimpse of the man out of the corner of her left eye as he dived into the ditch by the road-side, but it made her jump so that the car almost ran into the ditch too. Mrs Carpenter pushed the gear-stick away from her and pulled it into second with a crunching of metal cogs. And she accelerated away as fast as she could.

Capability Black lay on his face in the ditch with his finger ends biting hard into the grassy earth. A rivulet of water pushed coldly into his face and ran underneath him down the length of his body, which was stiff and trembling. He listened to the whine of the car engine as it was forced to peak revs and heard the breaks in the tone as the driver changed up, then up again, and the whine became a fading hum.

Another car came round the bend with headlights flicking, one, two—no! Only two. The engine noises died away and Capability became conscious of the church clock in its Norman tower looming over him. It had still not struck the half-hour. A feeling, partly like physical hunger and partly like fear, came over him and, as a man does who has given up smoking and is in his third week, he did confident inner battle with himself. Ten o'clock, he told himself. You had to have a plan and you had to stick to it. They all said so. So he would make his break across the road and through the timber yard at exactly ten o'clock.

Capability raised his head slightly and ducked down immediately as another car came round the bend with headlights on full beam and accelerated away up the straight. Four cars gone; the sports, the Mini, the Austin Cambridge and the big saloon he was not quite sure of. Looked a bit like a German job. Anyhow, there had been seven parked outside the visit-hut. That left the two Jaguars and the Humber. He felt a little warmer inside. This was planning all right.

He pushed himself on his side out of the water and pulled his wet shirt front and tunic away from his skin. Christ, what a mess. Another car was coming, a powerful car. Capability guessed a Jaguar. He rolled over again on to his stomach and pulled himself into the longer grass and rubbed his muddy hands over his face to darken the skin. The warm feeling was growing inside him. He flexed his thin shoulders and the big clock above him struck the half-hour with a rusty clank. The Jaguar, with only its sidelights showing, rolled quietly to a halt outside the church gate, thirty feet from where he lay.

Two screws got out of the car and went into the churchyard flashing their torches from side to side. The driver stayed behind the wheel and Capability saw a rough outline of the man's face as he struck a match and lit a cigarette. He watched the glow flare and fade as the man, one of the visitors, sucked at the cigarette. Then he buried his face in the ground and thought of Mavis. He had had one of her breasts in his hand in the visit-hut. The dirty bitch. He tried to push his body into the shelter of the soil.

It was not just the business with her bra and the way she had made a fuss about it so that the visit-screw had no option but to interfere. There was last week's letter. She had sat on Rod's knee at this club see, exclamation mark. Three ruddy exclamation marks. And who the bloody hell was Rod anyway, for Christ's sake? What a laugh it had been, exclamation mark, etc. Jackie and she got a bit tiddly, three exclamation marks. Charming. But that was not all.

There was a knot in Capability's stomach. He saw a man's hand on his wife's thigh and his wife was laughing. Like she had laughed in the visit-hut this afternoon as she pushed his hand away from her breast and said 'Don't be silly, Bern!' Except that that had been impatient laughter had it not? Capability's inner glow of adventure froze into his own terrible reality. She had engineered that row over her bra to get away sooner. It was obvious.

The man in the Jaguar tossed his cigarette out into the road and got out himself, stretching his arms and then shuddering noisily with the cold. Through the thick holly hedge Capability could see the two torches coming back towards the gate and he could hear the screws talking quietly to each other. The man from the car went to meet them at the gate and the three of them leant on the gate, whispering. The driver laughed out loud but broke the laugh off abruptly as if he had just remembered he was in church. The trio were still, only their heads moving as they peered around them into the darkness. One of the screws shone his torch idly along the ditch but the beam was too weak to reach Capability.

'He's miles away by now,' the screw said. 'They'll probably pick him up at home. The silly bastard's probably feeling randy.'

The driver made sympathetic noises in his throat and then coughed as if the noises embarrassed him. He shuddered with cold again as he held the back door of the Jaguar open for the two screws to get in. Then he got behind the wheel, backed in towards the church gate and drove back towards the prison.

The dirty cow had it coming to her. There was no clear idea in Capability's mind, but he knew he had to do something or go mad. The knot in his stomach had become an ache in his groin. His own hand was on his wife's white thigh. She wriggled away and said 'Don't be silly, Bern!' and there was the shadow of a man in the background. Capability screwed his eyes up and shook his head violently to shake away the images. Mavis was a dirty old cow. He knew it. He should have known it all along.

Through his angry tears Capability could see the lights of the prison a quarter of a mile away, the whole thing was lit up like an airport by the huge arc lights on the fences which swivelled round in widening and decreasing circles looking for a man who had strayed from the herd. Underneath Capability's anger and sorrow there was still something left of the warm glow of excitement. After all, this was all for him, Bern Black of Stepney. He knew little about anything except motors but he had started all this. Capability Bern Black. Christ knows why 'Capability' but that's what everybody called him. That toffy-nosed sod George had thought of it. Something to do with his vegetable patch.

The welfare officer that afternoon had not been able to follow Capability's reasoning. He had told Capability, in fact, that he considered Mavis to be a very fine girl and that he, Capability, was making something out of nothing. The tortured man had clutched at the welfare officer's regulation straw and had gone off to the bath-house wrapped in a warm glow of pride in his big-boned and faithful wife. Then, as he lay in his hot bath, he remembered that her letters had been getting shorter and shorter and that she had been smiling as she arrived at the visit-hut. Smiling at what? At who, for Christ's sake?

Evidence mounted. There was this bastard Rod who-ever he was and that fuss over her bra when there was no need for it. And just a minute. She'd been five minutes late for the visit and she'd said the bus had broken down. Mavis always called a motor a bus, he remembered now. So whose bloody motor? Rod's? Christ, that two-timing whore. In that moment he had decided to escape. By the time he had finished with Mavis nobody would want her.

One snip of the heavy wire-cutters and the diamond mesh behind the boiler-house ran up in a ladder like a snagged nylon stocking. Old Markham's snooker final was just beginning. The screws had just completed their eight o'clock patrol of the wires and would no doubt go inside to watch the snooker. He had watched the men carrying their boards and boxes of chessmen into the visit-hut and he had counted the cars in which the visitors arrived. He had a minimum of three-quarters of an hour before the count and he was missed, possibly an hour by the time the number of men playing chess had been rechecked and there had been two or three recounts in the dining-hall. It would take him ten minutes to reach the ditch by the church and he would wait there until the stroke of ten.

Capability skirted the big lettuce field and climbed the wall into the graveyard behind the church. The church itself was in darkness but the vicarage close by had a light burning in one of the upstairs windows. The vicar always went to bed early. Capability had helped once to clean the old church and the vicar had told him so. He liked to write in bed. Capability threaded his way through the gravestones to the gate, looking over his shoulder nervously at the tilting stones and blurred, railed crypts. He settled himself in the ditch to wait and think, or to try not to think.

Now he relaxed as the sound of the Jaguar faded into the distance and rolled on his side again out of the water. He strained his eyes up towards the clock in the tower but he could not be sure of the position of the hands. He reckoned it must be around twenty-five minutes to ten. The cold of the water from the little stream was striking through to his stomach and he felt as though he had insects crawling all over his body. He could not seem to get a picture of Mavis with clothes on into his mind. He felt sick. He rolled back into the water as another car came round the bend.

The clock on the dashboard of Mrs Carpenter's car said twenty-five minutes to ten as she drove into the garage and switched off the ignition. She was still trembling. She sat for some seconds with her hand on the door-catch. Why hadn't she stopped? Why hadn't she gone to a telephone box and called the prison? The picture of the tall man diving into the ditch was still clear in her mind, terrifying, pathetic. She knew nothing about him, not even his name or what he had done. The only thing of which she was sure was that she wished she had not seen him.

She got out of the car and walked slowly up to the house. She wished that John were not away tonight because she wanted to be told what to do. The house felt cold as she entered. In the darkness she bumped into the little hall-table which held the telephone and it tinkled as the receiver was rattled in its cradle. She put her hand down to steady it and snatched it as if it were hot. No. What did she know about the poor soul. She went into the lounge and sank wearily into an arm-chair. Her head was beginning to ache.

Tim and John would be very definite, of course. Both

in opposite directions. Tim would say let the poor fellow be, because locking people up was wrong like hanging people or staying married to people you didn't like. Mrs Carpenter smiled to herself as she remembered the unending but boisterous arguments between her son and her husband. A few weeks at a university, John had said, and any form of punishment was wrong. Only students were humane.

There had been a meeting in the village before the prison was opened and the Governor had come along to explain that no violent cases and no sexual offenders would be kept there. Most of the villagers had continued to object all the same but Mrs Carpenter spoke in support of the Governor because she believed that everybody was entitled to fresh air and decent surroundings and what did it matter if the value of their houses went down by a few hundred pounds.

Not long after the prison was opened, the Governor had asked her to form the chess circle and she had agreed immediately. John had said he thought it was a mistake but Tim had been enthusiastic. She had not liked it at first but gradually she learned to accept that she was wanted and unwelcome at the same time and, like James Markham, that you are supposed to laugh at tragic anecdotes. Eventually it came to be that she would let them all go because you could never be sure who was bad and who was just mistaken or had been led away by circumstances. It came to be that even Tim said he thought she was going a bit too far and one night he asked her what she would do if she knew where an escaped prisoner was hiding.

Mrs Carpenter had told her son she didn't know. She supposed it depended on what kind of a man he was. If he were just a thief she could not say what she would do. Perhaps she would speak to the man and tell him it would be better if he gave himself up. John had laughed and Tim had said that that laugh was typical of the hang-'em, flog-'em, jail-'em-and-be-damned brigade. Then they had all laughed together and put their arms around each other because they remembered something.

Now it *had* happened and Mrs Carpenter only knew that she wanted the man in the ditch to find some sort of happiness. But suppose he did something terrible? There were no known violent cases at the prison but who can tell what a man on the run will do if somebody stands in his way? She put her head in her hands and tried to remember what the man had looked like. He was tall. That was all she knew. He was tall and he had plunged head first into a ditch a little this side of the village church. Twenty minutes to ten. Dear God why did she have to see the poor soul. Why did it have to be her car that sent him scurrying to earth like a hunted animal. She wanted him to get away and be with his wife and children again. He was not doing anybody any harm.

The wives of the prison officers would have been in no doubt. Mrs Carpenter wished her mind was as clear as theirs. Perhaps it was because their husbands were what they were or perhaps it was just because they were the kind of women who married that manner of man but they seemed to live among it without even knowing it was there. They had a way of not looking at the men and of referring to them as if they were a football crowd. It was not purposeful indifference, that was easy to see. In this situation they would act immediately, without thinking. There would be no need to think.

Their children seemed cast in the same mould. They played by the prison wires as easily and uncaring as any child in any street. She had seen men speak to them playfully from inside the wires and the children had not replied or even looked towards the men. The children had not been ignoring the men. They had not even heard the words. It was as if it were the barking of a dog or the creaking of a tree in the wind, background noise to their play, not unusual enough to merit attention.

It was not that Mrs Carpenter did not know what was right and lawful. She knew she should have picked up the telephone seven minutes ago at twenty-five minutes to ten. But it was not what was lawful that she cared about. She wanted the man in the ditch to go free but first she wanted certain guarantees: that he would not hurt anybody, that he would not steal from anybody who was poor, or get any of his friends into trouble. Nobody could give her these guarantees so she sat with her aching head in her hands. She believed in

God and God was just. He had allowed her son to steal and escape punishment and He had allowed this man to go free. God did not forget. He wanted gratitude and He liked an eye for a tooth. She was fearful for her son because he was weak like her. God might not give him a third chance.

It was raining. Capability could feel the heavy drops on the side of his face as he tried to peer up into the darkness towards the clock tower. It seemed that he could see three hands against the discoloured white face of the clock but it looked like twenty to ten. His whole body was stiff with cold and he eased his stomach out of the water and massaged it with his right hand. The first Jaguar had come past again and the big Humber had gone as well.

That left only the other Jaguar and he wished to hell it would pass soon.

Capability was not angry any more and there was no picture in his mind of his naked wife. He had escaped. How many times had he said that escaping was crazy and that escaping for the sake of a woman was even crazier. But that was because he was secure in the knowledge that his wife was faithful. Not like some of those drabs he had seen at the visits.

He thought of his bed and his little vegetable patch behind the hut. Christ, he had enjoyed that bit of garden. The garden-screw had taught him a lot too. He was a decent bastard that one, even if he did keep joking that he hated cons. Not many people in Stepney had gardens. Bern Black certainly hadn't. He had not told Mavis but he wanted to move into the country when he got out. He had not told her because he was not sure how she would take it. She was a lively sort of girl. She had talked about opening a club.

Capability wanted to talk to Mavis. He wanted to look dirty and dishevelled and sad when he talked to her and he wanted her to cry and throw herself into his arms. He could feel the tears rising behind his eyes as he thought how cold he was and how misused.

The man would not be there. A man did not escape from prison and then lie in a ditch in the rain a few hundred yards away. Mrs Carpenter looked at her wrist watch. Seventeen minutes to ten. Good heavens, it was nearly a quarter of an hour since she had passed the church. The man would be at least a mile away. There was no point in ringing anybody.

She was surprised by her own relief. There was no point in not ringing for that matter. That way everybody's consciences would be clear. She would have done her duty but God would know she didn't try. Mrs Carpenter went out to the telephone in the hall and told the prison officer who answered that she had seen a man in prison uniform in a ditch a few yards her side of the gate to the village church.

CHAPTER 8

'Towrag Charlie hasn't got a son, you soft cow,' said
Bert. 'Bet the daft old goat still thinks it's for pissin'
with.' He looked to the old man for agreement and the
old man smiled back agreement. Bert liked to be right
and his temper seemed to be wearing a bit thin tonight.
He had already knocked down Old George, who was
only forty, because his immersion heater was not boiling the water fast enough for the tea. 'You b'guided
b'me.' Bert waved a threatening finger at Sam, who was
saying it was a son of a bitch. 'That lad were no son of
Towrag's. He were one of them bloody God-botherers
from that fuckin' seminary.' He shoved Sam down onto
one of the lavatories and Sam said he didn't give a shit

for the son of a bitch, did he. The old man made to leave but Bert said he was to stay and have his tea. It would warm his bones up.

Bert had an ugly expression on his big friendly face. He sat in one of the handbasins with his legs swinging. 'I hope the bastard gets clear.' Bert looked at them all in turn and the old man knew it was a challenge to disagree and not just a statement. 'Whoever the bastard is I hope the bastard gets free. God help the poxy cow whoever he is.' He looked down at his swinging feet. 'Five years.' Bert looked up quickly at Old George and told him to mash the tea whether the water was boiling or not. 'The bastard screws'll be round in ten minutes, you cow.' He looked down at his feet again, kicking the toes of his boots together pettishly. 'That's what I got. Five fuckin' years for a parcel of socks. Framed me, the bastards.'

The old man had heard the story a hundred times. The last time it had been a packet of handkerchiefs and the time before a carton of two hundred cigarettes. In the dimmer past he thought he could remember it being a crate of gin. The only unchanging part of the story was that Bert had been framed by the police, which, of course, was exactly the case with everybody else. What the old man could not understand was why it was only the offence for which they were currently under sentence of which they were innocent.

He knew Bert's criminal record better than Scotland Yard. On the previous occasion he had been convicted for warehouse breaking, an offence of which he was now merrily guilty. The old man wondered if they waited until the day they were released to finally admit their guilt of the last offence or whether they waited until they came in the next time on a framed charge. He held out his mug while Old George filled it with watery tea. He wondered what Bert's wife was like. Bert had mentioned her on several occasions. 'The old bag,' he had said. God, what a life for a woman. The old man knew Bert had two brothers. One in Winson Green and the other in Walton.

The screws would be up late tonight. It could be George who was away. The old man had been to his room and he was not there. He didn't tell the others, why should he? They were so damned smart they could find out for themselves. He was surprised, in fact, that they didn't know already. There must be a block in the grapevine. Probably the screws were feeling too peevish to part with any information.

Bert was really in a bad humour. The old man had seen him this way on several occasions but tonight he seemed to be particularly truculent. They tried so hard to pretend they didn't really care but every now and again the years loomed up before and behind them and caught them off balance. The old man wondered if on these occasions they weighed the easy money against the years in limbo but he thought not. They had too much pride for that. Too much pride even ever to admit to themselves that they might have been wrong. Even once.

Not all of them, of course. Just the Berts. There was another man in the lavatory tonight who said it was not worth it. He said it was full of good intentions. He was not one of the usual party but Old George had invited him in for a cup of tea because it was his last night. Old George wished now that he hadn't and so did the old man. There was going to be trouble. Bert was pushing for a fight. But the man, Flint, was in a joyous world of his own. The welfare officer had fixed him up with a dish-washing job at a local holiday camp. Eight pounds a week all found. He would have a chalet of his own with a radio and a day and a half off a week. Only seasonal, mind you, but he would have the job to look forward to every spring. If a bloke saved right he could last out the winter nicely. Christ, yes.

Bert slammed the metal heels of his boots together. 'Some people don't know what bird is.' He was looking at Sam seated on the lavatory but he was talking at Flint. 'Some bastards could tack their little bit of porridge on to th'end of mine and I'd never even know the difference.' Bert looked at the old man with some sort of angry, injured pride in his eyes and then across at Flint who had not stopped talking. He shouted this time. 'Some lousy gas-meter bandits don't know what bird is!' Bert was off the handbasin and he had his face pressed up close to Flint's. 'You talk about porridge, you bastards! What porridge have you done, you cow? What fuckin' porridge have you done? Eh?'

Flint backed off to the wall. He was scared. 'Not

much, Bert. Not like you have, Bert. Christ no.'

Bert had a fistful of the man's collar and was pushing his head against the tiled wall. 'You talk about bird, you cows. What bird have you bastards done? I can tell you poxy bastards about bird! Dartmoor!' He spat the word into Flint's face. 'Parkhurst! The 'ville! Walton!' He cracked Flint's head against the tiles. 'You talk about bird, you bastards. What do you towrag cunts know about bird? Tell me! Tell me!' He rammed Flint's head against the tiles. The old man and Old George started to move towards the door but Bert saw them. 'Stay where you are! Stay just where you are. Flint here's got to tell us about his bird. Ever done time on the Moor, Flint?'

Flint's head cracked hard against the tiles again. 'No, Bert. Never been to the Moor. Sorry.'

Bert swung the man away from the wall and slammed him against the urinal opposite. He pushed him until he was sitting in the urinal. 'Think you've done bird, eh?' Bert was almost screaming. 'Ever done a stretch at the 'ville, Flint?' He gave the man no time to answer. He pulled him up out of the urinal and flung him across into the toilet where Sam was sitting. Sam was knocked on to the floor and Bert kicked him in the stomach.

He had Flint by the back of his collar and was ramming his head down into the lavatory bowl, trying to force his face into the narrow well of water. The old man could hear Flint's screams, muffled and echoing in the porcelain bowl. Bert was in a frenzy. 'Tell us about your bird, Flint! Tell us, you bastard!' He pulled the lavatory seat down, trapping Flint's neck underneath it, and sat on it, jumping up and down. 'Porridge, you bastard! What do you know about porridge? Tell us, you cunt!' He pulled Flint out of the lavatory and let him sag to the floor. The man's face was blue and Bert lifted his boot and held it over the unconscious face. He looked at Old George and the old man and lowered his foot to the floor. 'To hell with the poxy cow. Clear those tea-leaves up, George. The bastard screws'll be up in a minute!' He took the old man's arm and led him out into the corridor and along to his room. 'Get to bed, Jimmy.' He opened the door for the old man and closed it quietly after him.

Flint opened his eyes and saw a pair of shining boots a few inches from the end of his nose. He closed his eyes quickly and braced himself for the kick. 'No, please! Please!' He formed the words at the back of his throat but he heard his own voice only as a croak. His eyes were screwed up tightly. Balls of blackness seemed to shoot up from somewhere around the base of his neck and into the top of his skull where they dispersed into millions of darting pin-pricks of light. His mouth was full of dozens of pieces of broken dentures but he could not spit them out. His lips felt like huge layers of spongy rubber. He could not move them because his nose seemed to be rammed down on top of them like a wedge. 'Please! Please!' The shattered dentures rattled in his mouth. He was all head. Just a big ball of pain waiting to be kicked.

He could feel a pair of hands at his throat but they were gentle hands. Then somebody said, 'Take it easy mate.' The hands lifted his head and pushed something soft between his head and the tiled floor. Flint opened his eyes again. The boots were still there but now they did not look like kicking boots. They were new and creased uncomfortably behind the toe-caps like new boots in a squatting position. A trouser leg brushed against his face. Grey. Flint closed his eyes and opened them again. Yes, grey. He raised his eyes slowly and painfully up the grey trouser leg and saw a dark blue jacket with silver buttons and a little chain hanging from one of the breast pockets. Christ, half a screw. Where in hell's name was he?

'Take it easy mate. You'll be all right.' Flint's eyes travelled up past the jacket to the face. He had seen that face somewhere. Where? It was a young face, and worried. Christ, yes. It was the new screw who arrived yesterday. Longshanks. They couldn't find a pair of trousers to fit him. Flint closed his eyes again. Thank Christ for that. Another kick would have been just about the poxy end.

The tall screw took his cap from under Flint's head and put it on his own, keeping Flint's head off the floor with his left hand. He grinned at the man on the floor. 'Let's get you out of here. We'll get you down to the sick bay and then we'll get the doctor and the Governor to sort this thing out.' Oh, Christ. Here we go again. Where were you on the night of the ninth at nine o'clock et fucking cetera?

They shuffled along the corridor, Flint with his arm around Longshanks's shoulders. He could see lights under the doors along the corridor but there were no sounds from any of the rooms. All earwigging behind the doors though, the bastards. Someone would do that bastard Bert one of these days. Three years to do. Serve the bastard right. He hoped he rotted in hell.

It never occurred to Flint to question why Bert had beaten him. If he had been forced to answer the question he would probably have said Bert felt like it, he supposed. Flint had done more bird than Bert and everybody knew it, including Bert. But if Flint had let his mind dwell on the subject, which he did not, he would have said that that had nothing to do with it. It was a beating which stood alone without reason or consequences and which would be measured only in the degree of its severity.

Longshanks helped him on to the couch in the sick bay and telephoned the main guardroom to say that he had found an inmate called Flint lying unconscious and badly beaten on the floor of the lavatory. What should he do? Longshanks listened for a few moments, then put the telephone down. He went to a cupboard by the wall and took out some bottles and some cotton wool and brought them over to the couch.

'The doctor will be here in a minute with the Governor.' He patted Flint playfully on the arm. 'They're going to want to know what happened, you know.'

And you can say that again, sonny. They never gave up when it came to wanting to know. Stick around for half an hour or so and you'll see how it works. It was a performance older than the floral dance which you could see gentlemen perform at Eton. The code of something or other invented by bullies for the protection of bullies. Everybody was required to play the game, a three-sided contest between the victor, the victims, and the screws. There was only ever one winner.

Longshanks gave a half-shamefaced salute as the Governor and the doctor came into the sick bay. The doctor was a small fat man in a shabby suit. He wore a shabby shirt and tie and a face made shabby by years of looking for pains in healthy chests. They said that Doctor Fitzgibbon only treated the dead but they were exaggerating. He had reached the stage though where be believed nothing that didn't scream aloud in agony, and he was not altogether sure about that any more. He had just under a year to go to his retirement and he was dog-tired.

He pushed Flint's beaten head to one side and back again with a limp, flabby hand. He pulled the eyelids back and Flint winced. 'Quite a mess,' he said, speaking to the wall beyond the couch. He turned to the Governor and said they would have to have an X-ray of this man's head and chest. They would need an ambulance to take this man to the City Hospital. This man was hurt.

The chief came in and looked at Flint on the couch and then to the Governor. 'They picked him up near the church, sir. He's in your office.'

The Governor grunted. Flint could see that he was angry. 'Get an ambulance for this man, chief. He has to go to hospital.' The chief left and the Governor pulled a chair up by the couch. He rested his elbow on the couch and put his chin in his hand.

'You ran into a door?'

Flint said that that was so. Longshanks had removed his broken dentures but there were still small pieces left in his mouth which rattled uncomfortably against his gums when he spoke. He wanted to go to sleep. So did the Governor. It had been a hell of a day.

'Right, we'll start at the beginning. Which door was it?' Flint let out a croak of protest as the doctor dabbed a stinging liquid on to a cut in his forehead.

'The lavatory door, sir.' Round one and all square.

'How did it happen?'

Flint thought for a moment. 'I thought it was open, sir. But it was closed.'

The Governor said he understood, but the injuries seemed to be extensive.

'Yes, sir. I was running, sir.' Next question, please.

Let me see. Yes, witnesses. 'Was anybody else there when you ran into the closed door?'

Flint considered. 'I don't think so, sir. Not that I can remember, sir. I was dazed.'

The Governor said he was not surprised. This officer here had said that he, Flint, was unconscious.

'Oh no, sir. Not unconscious. No, sir. Dazed.' That would be the preliminaries. The Governor would now sharpen his attack.

'Who did it?'

Christ that was cunning. 'What do you mean, sir?'

'It was plain enough,' the Governor said. Lavatory doors did not inflict multiple injuries.

'No, sir.' A pause.

The Governor lit a cigarette. 'Well?'

Flint said he must have fallen on the floor then.

The Governor took a turn round the room and sat down again. 'We'll try again,' he said. 'Now, were you going in or coming out when you ran into the lavatory door?' The Governor leaned back in his chair.

Oh, the cunning old cow. Flint could feel himself smiling and he wondered what his face looked like. 'Out, sir.' Ha, that had foxed the cunning old cow. 'The door opens inwards, sir.'

The Governor took another turn round the room and stopped to say something to Longshanks. Flint could not hear what they were saying but Longshanks left the room and the Governor came back to the couch.

He leaned closer to Flint. 'Now let us see how funny you think this is. We can't let you go until you're physically fit.' He leaned back in his chair again and lit another cigarette. He could see something changing in Flint's face but he was not sure exactly what it meant. He had not wanted to say that but he had a report to make to the Home Office.

What a day. A punch-up in the dining-hall, Jenkins's unexplained black eye and black nose, two abortive escapes and now a man beaten to within a couple of inches of his life. And here, in the name of God. Years of work were at stake. It had taken years to convince the local inhabitants that the kind of men he brought here did not escape. It had taken more years to convince the Home Office that his kind of men did not beat each other. What in God's name made a man protect another who had tried to kill him? It was not love or even the barest affection. It was not even regard. It must be fear then. But why this man? He was getting out. What had this man to fear from the man who attacked him?

Flint was trying to work it out. He would be in the City Hospital until he was better and then he would be free. The police didn't want him for any previous job, he was sure of that. Why not tell the bastards? He owed that Bert something, for Christ's sake.

What about the job? He remembered the job with a pang of fear. 'What about the job, sir? The job at the holiday camp?'

The Governor said he was sorry, and he was. He had a feeling about Flint. He had a feeling that this time he might have made it. The man had had enough. 'I'm afraid the job is out, Flint. They want a man immediately and you don't look like being fit for several weeks. The welfare officer will try somewhere else.' He could see the confusion in Flint's face, the bitter disappointment. Then the anger, which was what he wanted to see. He wanted Flint to be angry enough for anything.

Nobody knew how much he wanted that job, the chalet, with his own radio and eight pounds a week all found. It was all he had ever wanted. Now it was gone because Bert had smashed him. He owed Bert something all right. He owed him a lifetime in hell, the lousy pig.

The welfare officer wouldn't find him another job, not like that one with his own chalet and radio and a chance to save a bit of money. It had taken him two years to swing the holiday camp job and even then the manager hadn't really wanted a man from the prison. He was on trial, the welfare officer had said. Whatever he did would reflect on the chances of men coming after. And Flint had meant to try. He had promised the welfare officer he would not fail him and he had meant it.

Flint did not hesitate because he was not sure what Bert deserved. He was battling against a lifetime of tradition. He wanted also to get his story right because he wanted to include the fact that Bert was a baron and that he had punched Jenkins in the dining-hall this evening. He also wanted to say that Bert was a queer, which was not true. In his mind he compiled a list of

Bert's offences against humanity, true and false. The fact that he had a half-bottle of gin hidden in a plant pot in his room and the lie that Bert was planning to escape.

'What about it now, Flint?' The Governor tried not to make his voice too eager. 'This man's done you harm, whoever he is. You can have my word for it that he will never know who told. He'll be back in a closed prison by tomorrow afternoon. As soon as you tell us who he is we'll lock him up for the night. You'll be in the City Hospital anyway.' He didn't like what he was doing but there was no other way. 'You're not coming back, you know that. I don't want to see you in here again.'

Flint was including everybody in his list. All the barons, all the tobacco carriers, the bent screws, Old George and his immersion heater. The whole bastard lot of them were going to get what they deserved and they could blame it all on Bert. They could beat him until he was crippled and make sure the day never came when he got out. To hell with the whole crew of dead-beats.

The chief came in and stood behind the Governor's chair. He reminded Flint of a policeman he had once known, a bull from Salford who had arrested him for receiving. Seven years for that lot and twenty-six other offences taken into consideration. Or was it twenty-five? He couldn't remember. It must have been at least fifteen years ago.

Had he included the Newcastle job? He must have

done, for Christ's sake. Twenty-six or twenty-five. What did it matter. The Judge hadn't even listened when the Salford bull droned through the list. He had only heard the number. 'Very impressive record,' the bloody old coot had said.

The Newcastle job was quite a big one as he remembered it. Fifty thousand cigarettes it was. Had he asked for it to be included?

The Governor and the chief were both standing over him. Just look at them, for Christ's sake. A couple of bloody vultures. The chief looked as if he was going to speak but the Governor nudged him with his elbow. That was queer. Why didn't he want the chief to speak? Did the chief know something about the Newcastle job?

If the law still had the Newcastle job on their books they could be waiting for him outside. These bastards wouldn't tell him. Not if they wanted him to tell about Bert they wouldn't. They would have him back inside and Bert would be waiting for him to swash his face into a lavatory and to kick him as he lay on the floor. They thought they had him there, didn't they? The cunning bastards really thought they had him going. Just look at the chief. He's just about ready to burst, the stupid old goat.

'I ran into a door, sir. I thought it was open.' That was all they were getting. Flint wasn't going to grass on anybody. Certainly not on Bert. These bastards couldn't beat it out of him. It was a code, after all. Like they have at Eton.

The Governor turned away and pulled the chief with him. It was no good, he said. They would try along the corridor in the morning but they knew how far that would get them. He told the chief to get the men to bed. It was after ten.

He had never wanted to be a Governor. He had taken the job when he came out of the Army because there did not seem to be anything else. All the same he had given it everything he had because he was that kind of man.

The Governor was ashamed of his job. Not because he thought it was an inferior way of earning a living but because he knew the ordinary man and woman in the street looked on it as something vaguely unwholesome.

They did not say so directly, of course. They merely implied that their sympathies were with the underdog and that a man had to be pretty desperate for a crust to take it up. No, it was not really true to say that he was ashamed. It embarrassed him to admit in public what he did for a living.

They always began by saying that they knew nothing about it, which, in general, they didn't. Then they had opinions on how prisoners should be treated; harshly, gently and even not at all. They had opinions on prison officers which also varied according to the colour of their politics but which generally came down to the conclusion that they were lazy men, men who either didn't have enough brain power to push a pen or enough backbone to swing a pick. Then they had convictions.

The convictions varied like the opinions, but generally only two ways. There were the lock-'em-up-and-be-damneds and the let-'em-all-gos. Neither side knew anything about it, as they had already said, but they were firmly convinced that the only way to treat an old lag was to have him put down or to give him a three thousand a year job with responsibility. Crime would suffer, they said. The public were entitled to protection. The public did not take enough interest. It was obvious, surely.

Finally they had bias, these people who didn't know anything about it. They admitted their bias. They boasted about their bias, which they asked everybody to respect even if they were fool enough not to agree with it. They had bias because they had a friend whose daughter had been raped by a man who got off scot-free. Or they had bias because they had a friend, just an acquaintance, really, who served a short term for a minor motoring offence and was brutally beaten in his cell by criminals or sadistic prison officers. One had to make allowances but there was no doubt that the whole prison system needed shaking up. You had to be harder and softer and kinder and more cruel and quicker. It was no good building more comfortable prisons and it was no good leaving men in damp dungeons or giving them fresh air or depriving them of fresh air or feeding them or starving them or letting them have visitors or turning it into a home-from-home. None of that was any good. You had to have discipline and a relaxed atmosphere. Give them a little money but don't pay them. Let them do a worthwhile job of work making things which could be sold so that they could pay for their keep and have a pride in themselves, but don't let them run foul of the trade unions. We don't see where the difficulty lies. Of course we don't know anything about it really. You chaps have to live with it.

The Governor walked along by the wires with his hands in his pockets. It had been a day and a half all right and all to be sorted out tomorrow. He waved to the men in the guardroom and climbed into his car. For a while there he had thought Flint was going to make it. But not now. He was a goner and no mistake. He would be back inside three months.

CHAPTER 9

Trouble in South Vietnam. Trouble in the Congo.
Trouble in Malaysia. Somebody ought to do something
about that fellow Sukarno the old man thought. Somebody ought to do something about those rebels in
Albertville as well and those Viet-Cong. What a bloody
crazy world. Why didn't they put something cheerful
in the paper just by way of a change. Murder in Ken-
sington; fire in Glasgow, two dead; Wilson accuses,
Heath accuses, Grimond accuses; mother dies in triple
road smash, road deaths up. Here's a gem: fifteen years
for man who wouldn't learn. He could hear Sam cursing
on one side and Bert coughing on the other. They
would be round tomorrow to find out about Flint.

They ought to hang Bert because he was a mad dog.

The old man threw his *Daily Telegraph* on to the floor and picked up his books. He put them back on the bedside locker without opening them. He had better get his pyjamas on. The screw would be round in a minute to switch the lights off. The screw would be round to put them to bed like infants, to switch out the lights and say 'No talking'. When he had been to all the rooms he would stand at the end of the corridor and listen as a mother does. He would hear Sam talking to himself and he would shout 'Shut up!' as even mothers do sometimes when it has been a very bad day. This had been a terrible, terrible day.

The old man pushed himself into a sitting position and gasped with the pain in his chest. God, that was a bad one. Please God, not now. Just a few months. The old man hunted feverishly in his mind for a prayer, any prayer. He half remembered a prayer from his childhood and he said what he knew of it to himself, rushing through the words. The squeezing pain began to subside and after a few moments he pulled off his clothes and put on his pyjamas. Gently he slipped his old white legs under the blankets and lowered himself down on to the pillow. He let his breath escape slowly, gratefully. The pain was fading away leaving behind it a numbness in his chest. He stared up at the yellow ceiling. A tiny crack in the plaster above his head had lengthened, he was sure of it. He looked for the face in the little jagged crack but he couldn't find it. He had seen it the night before, distinctly. The craggy forehead and the hooked nose and the jutting upper lip. The mouth had never been very distinct but the chin showed boldly, a big chin with a little goatee beard. None of them were there now. He couldn't even find the nose. The old man screwed his eyes up and peered at the crack section by section. Damn it, the nose had gone. His eyes blurred with staring and he closed them and allowed his thin body to sag into the mattress.

Jane would be making herself a cup of hot chocolate before going to bed. Tom would be at the 'Barley Mow' telling funny stories. They were only vague thoughts flitting through the old man's mind, which was tired beyond caring. He heard the screw open the door and flick off the light and say good night and he replied mechanically. He didn't think about freedom because he didn't care. His thin old body was numb and his mind was slipping into oblivion. A film strip drifted through his semi-conscious mind: Jenkins without hate, Bert smiling and friendly, he and George sitting in the cubby-hole drinking coffee. The pictures blurred around the edges and disappeared.

James Hubert Markham was asleep. His body hardly made a bulge in the blankets and his absence was felt hardly at all in the outside world. Tomorrow he would begin again. Perhaps.

THE END